Do Over

Carol Anne Leathers

Illustrations by

Stephanie Lynn Leathers

Based on drawings by

Terri Mills

and photographed by

Steve Lemioux

Library of Congress Control Number:		2012916345
ISBN:	Hardcover	978-1-4797-1083-6
	Softcover	978-1-4797-1082-9
	Ebook	978-1-4797-1084-3

To order additional copies of this book, contact:
Xlibris Corporation
1-888-795-4274
www.Xlibris.com
Orders@Xlibris.com
114756

Do Over

FOREWORD FROM THE AUTHOR

This is actually the final thing I am writing just prior to the time of publication, but it is important and is most appropriate to be placed here.

Prior to moving to the final publication of this book, I asked that a professional critique be made of an earlier version of the manuscript with the purpose being to guide me as an author in making *Do Over* the best that it could be. I must have misunderstood the purpose for this review as the response by whoever the reviewer is was not only negative and unconstructive but scathing and quite malicious.

Do Over is a story about child abuse and surviving the very long-term effects of child abuse. It is my first book but did not begin as a book or even a plan for a book. In truth, it began as a journal, a way to express a tremendous feeling of sadness, hopelessness, and grief starting with what had long been suppressed during a time in this author's life when it was really needed, what in hindsight I now understand was a true crossroad for me.

*   *   *

In the critique, I was accused of insulting the reader's intelligence with the idea of there being truth and fiction with only the author knowing which is which. Furthermore, the critique essentially indicated that I had no right to speak on the subject of child abuse and essentially rendered the abuse cited in the book as a sister being angry with a brother. Obviously, this particular critic, whoever he or she was, did not read the book.

First of all, I would never knowingly attempt to insult any potential reader, period. The beginning of the book was in fact the beginning of the journal on the first night of writing, long before the journal became a book, long before contemplating publication, and long before its many rewrites. It reflected the very deep sadness I felt at that time, and I have left it there for that reason and because it led me to creating the character of Reb and telling my story through her. Most of the original journal is gone now, but the initial paragraph remains as a reminder of where the book started.

Second, the child abuse and injuries incurred by Reb are absolutely true, brutally true. The abuse really happened, and they are my injuries, all of them. The child abuse suffered by Reb's siblings is also true.

What have been changed are names, dates, and places, with certain events changed or fictionalized and with many places not specifically named at all. Of course, Reb's "do over" is totally fictional.

*   *   *

Reb's thoughts, decisions, and even her rambling and sometimes ranting is her way of coming to grips with what was and wasn't because of her history of child abuse and are only one person's thoughts, one person's anguish, and one person trying to find her way, trying to understand, trying to heal and move on with her life. It is in no way meant to represent other people who have lived through child abuse. It is only one example.

For the critic who thought that this author had no right to express herself on the matter of child abuse, let me say this. The people who have lived through this type of adversity, no matter what the specifics, are experts in their own right, not a critic like you who thinks it is your function to decide on what one should or should not say or how one should say it. I lived through it. You (this particular critic) may not like the way I chose to tell the story, but yes, I do have a right to tell it.

Finally, this particular critic, whoever he or she is, makes a reference to this author as being a "religious woman" in a manner that is easily interpreted as derogatory and truly quite unflattering. That is fine, and this person is entitled to his or her opinion as to religion.

I am a Christian, albeit a very imperfect one. I am a Christian and have no reservation in stating so. God has been and will continue to be a tremendous influence on my life, and I have no reservation in saying that as well.

ACKNOWLEDGMENTS

First and foremost, to my very special parents who understood what it took for their daughter to heal and for always believing in me no matter what. Without them, this book would not have been published.

To my husband for a lifetime of love and acceptance.

To my son for being my inspiration to survive.

And most of all, to "Sissy" and "Sammy." This book is dedicated to you, my precious sister and brother, who shared the childhood journey, survived your own version of the abuse, and went on to be an inspiration to me.

DO OVER

Carol Anne Leathers

This is a work in progress. Let's see how it goes, write from my heart, and see how it goes. September 20, 2011, three days before my fifty-first birthday. This writing is dedicated to all of us who have been through the worst of abuse, survived, and not passed on the abuse to the next generation.

Do Over is a story about wishes and wanting a life different from what you have. It is a mixture of me and fiction, maybe more fiction than me, maybe more me than fiction, but again, we'll see where this takes me, hopefully to a point and place of greater understanding, acceptance, and appreciation. In the end, however, I am the only one who will know what is truth and what is fiction.

REB

"I know I ask perfection of a quite imperfect world and am fool enough to think that's what I'll find."

—The Carpenters

• •

If I could turn back time, if I could find a way . . . This song by Cher, she couldn't remember any other lines from it, had been playing and replaying in her head over the last couple of weeks, the thought for much longer. She wondered how many people had ever wondered if they could just go back and do it all over again, knowing what they knew but starting out with a clean slate. She had. Here she was, just a few days before her fifty-first birthday, feeling down, trying to remain hopeful, often hopeless, always tired, and inevitably disappointed with her life and where she was in the moment, but still trying. A long time ago, someone told her that when you work hard and try, really try, life gets better as you get older. Maybe it was something her parents had tried to teach her. Maybe it was something she had gleaned from TV or the movies. For whatever reason, she honestly could not remember who said this to her. She only knew that she had grown up with the notion and had believed it, counted on it. She should have known better.

Her name was Reb. She was born on September 23, 1960, the fourth and youngest child of two parents born in rural Maine during the depression. Reb is short for Rebecca, not Becky, but Reb. Reb chose this name just to be a little different, not the typical name for Rebecca, a name that stated, well, she really didn't know what it stated; she just liked the sound of it better than Becky. Back in the early days of the Internet, Reb's first e-mail address was "Pudge Reb." Most people whom she chatted with thought that her name meant that she was a fat rebel. It was hysterical to her as she was neither obese nor a rebel. In truth, Pudge was the name of her first Persian cat, a breed that she dearly loved, and Reb, well, Reb was both short for Rebecca and was her nickname.

* * *

Reb was born, raised, and had lived her entire life in Maine, a truly beautiful state that had everything most people would want. Later in life, she would do a limited amount of traveling, each to a place that she loved and was truly mesmerized with, places such as Canada, Niagara Falls, Bermuda, Key West, Disney World, Tampa, and the Carolinas. But, it was Maine that was home and had everything that any traveler could want, except maybe the winters which could be long and harsh.

Maine was a large state that from southern to northern tip took more than nine hours to drive by car. Northern Maine was full of small towns, none large, with mile upon mile of wilderness, some untamed and virgin, and beautiful pristine rivers such as the Allagash and the Saint John's. Before that was the incredibly beautiful Baxter State Park complete with magnificent moose and other wildlife in and around ponds and lakes, trail after trail and majestic mountains that on a rare clear day a snowcapped peak could be seen, including the tallest one in Maine, Mount Katahdin. To the west was Moosehead Lake, a huge intricately woven body of water that had to be seen to be appreciated.

Maine was bordered to the west and north by Canada and for a good portion of the state to the east as well. Beginning around Eastport and heading south, Maine was bordered by the Atlantic Ocean. From that point on, Maine was peppered with beautiful, sometimes quaint seaside towns, ports, and bays, with the most well-known being Bar Harbor in Acadia National Park. Acadia National Park was another incredible place to visit, both for tourists and Mainers. It was a place of such incredible beauty, a place of mountains, lakes, the ocean littered with islands, beaches, clam flats, Thunder Hole, forests, and miles and miles of roads and trails for the bikers and the hikers. All these places had been lovingly protected and maintained so that they remained without the taint of pollution, human and otherwise.

One of Reb's favorite seaside towns was Boothbay Harbor, a town that was similar to Bar Harbor and much further south, a town that she had first traveled to with her sister, the husbands, and her niece. Like Bar Harbor's whale watching tours, which were awesome, Boothbay offered short cruises around the local islands to view the wildlife and ocean life and the many landmarks. On these, it wasn't unusual to have a dolphin or two trailing along for the ride. Reb's favorite place of all was a tiny little island called Cabbage Island, a place where your lunch was cooked right on the beach in the seaweed and was the most delicious and authentic Maine seafood meal in the state, haddock chowder, two lobsters, steamed clams, baked potato, corn on the cob, blueberry cake, and a boiled egg. In later years when Reb's parents were elderly, she, her sister, the husbands, and her niece had taken her parents on this afternoon cruise and seaside dinner. At the time, her mother's health was such that she was wheelchair bound, and so they lifted her on to the boat and then on the island by hand. Her parents had loved the cruise. Her mother, a finicky eater by nature, when served her meal did not speak or take her eyes off the dinner until every bite was gone.

In the western part of Maine near the Canadian border was another area of incredible beauty and another area introduced to Reb and her husband by Reb's sister, the Rangeley Lake area complete with the western mountains and some of the most beautiful campgrounds in the state, campgrounds so coveted that reservations were made far in advance and the most desired weeks and spots took years to get. There was a time when once a year, Reb's sister, her sister's husband, their daughter, and a variety of their friends would camp out for one week in June, just before the official start of the tourist season at the South Arm campground on Richardson Lake. In time, Reb and her husband would be brought into the fold, and it would become a yearly tradition for them as well, at least for a few years.

Just outside of the campground, there is a very special little place, off the beaten path, looking almost like it didn't belong there yet for some reason had been put there by some unseen and unknown hand. It was a place found quite by accident by one of her sister's friends and shared with all, including Reb and her husband. Just off one of the many, many dirt paths leading into the woods was a narrow grassy and bushy path that if followed led to a giant cavern with levels and levels of rocks, gentle waterfalls, and a stream. It was a place that seemed out of place, and Reb wondered what the mystery was that had made it. Once at the bottom and with the sunlight filtering in, Reb felt as if she were in a different world, if not magical, certainly peaceful and a reminder of the hand that could make such beautiful things.

• •

There was little that truly could be considered urban in Maine. Yes, there was Portland, Maine's largest city and the wealthiest, and in it was most of what the city-type person would need or want, and even if there were places in it that had its history and charm, it didn't have the excitement of Boston or New York. There were also the smaller cities including Lewiston, Augusta, and Bangor. Of any of Maine's few cities, Augusta was by far the prettiest. It was also the capital and was a beautiful area geographically. Bangor was one of the oldest cities, born out of the logging industry and steadily growing. Lewiston, well, Lewiston was often referred to as the armpit of Maine. She didn't really know why; it just was, and Reb knew nothing more about it. In any case, Reb had grown up in one of these cities yet at heart was not a city girl and had no desire to be one.

Reb was by nature a country girl, a small-town girl, so Maine was for her the right place to be. If short on cities, Maine was peppered with towns. Maine was a state of towns. The many towns were truly the backbone of the state. To Reb, Maine's towns were fascinating because each town took on a different flavor and look depending on where it was.

Coastal towns had the coastal architecture, the places that were often described as quaint by outsiders. Many of the residents of the coastal towns worked hard in the tourist industry, often seven days a week during the warmer seasons so that there would be enough money earned to get through the long hard winters when the tourists disappeared. The fisherman and lobsterman worked year-round during the best fishing times no matter how brutal the conditions. These were often the people with the thick Maine accent that the rest of the country believed all Maine residents shared.

Then, there were the southern towns, the larger and wealthier towns, partly because people made better salaries in these areas and partly because the state tax base shifted heaviest in their direction. This was the part of the state that had the best roads, the most people, the more modern and expensive schools, some of the priciest homes, and a wealthier population that sometimes thought they were superior to their central and northern Maine counterparts. Reb remembered one time in recent years when she had been forced to travel to southern Maine in a terrible snowstorm, something she was petrified of doing. It was a Sunday, and the plows were not doing their job. In actuality, the plows in her area did no job at all.

As she traveled down the highway in white-out conditions, the highway remained unplowed, unplowed for about sixty miles, unplowed until she got to the city of Augusta, the capital. From that point on, the highways and all the roads she traveled were plowed and sanded. It was the same when she traveled back home. The roads were plowed and sanded until she got to Augusta, and then she was again on treacherous roads until she got home. Reb went away from that experience with a strong impression that for some reason, the lives of the people in the central and northern parts of the state somehow were not as valued as the people in the south.

Next, there were the towns in the north, many of which Reb had never visited. In this part of the state, there were huge areas of land that were considered unnamed townships or simply unnamed territories. Even along the only highway in the north, you would drive for miles and miles and see nothing but forest and what few towns you passed were gone in a blink. There were towns with fewer than one hundred people. Houses were often old and dilapidated. Stores and gas stations were few and far between. Schools were consolidated from many towns and were the poorest in the state as were most of the people who lived in these places. Of course, there were a few larger towns and small cities such as Houlton and Calais, but by and large, this enormous area of the state was sparsely populated and very poor. It was here that the Maine potato industry was the strongest, the farms giant, with even the schools closing during the harvest. Still, for many, it was difficult to eke out a living, yet most of these people were tough, resilient, and somehow found a way to survive and live in what really was a beautiful place.

Finally, there was central Maine which, for Reb, also included the western part of the state. It was in central Maine that Reb had grown up and made her lifelong home. This was also peppered with many towns of varying sizes. Geographically, it had its occasional small mountain and was dotted with dozens of lakes, ponds, rivers, and streams, some still pristine and some now polluted and not what they had been in Reb's childhood or, for that matter, in her parents'. In this central part of the state, what was most notable and what Reb loved the most were the miles and miles of rolling hills, the farms, fields, and woods. Reb loved the farms most. There were so many different kinds. Dairy farms, chicken farms, horse farms, even a farm near her that specialized in raising a special kind of small red deer. There were potato farms, corn, strawberries, apples, peas, string beans, cabbage, onions, squash, and pumpkin. The fields were harvested for the hay that would later be winter meals for the cows, goats, and horses. At the age of twelve, Reb had even worked on a farm that grew Chinese cabbage and pea pods. You name it and somewhere in Maine someone grew it. Reb loved the Farmer's markets and, at least for a time, grew some of her own stuff.

As for the people of central Maine, there were more of them than in the north and less of them than in the south. There were a few wealthy and a few poor with a larger number in the middle. In recent times, with the economy in such a bad state, there were now more of the poor with a homeless population that was growing. Many of the newly poor had once been part of the middle. In better economic times, the towns surrounding Bangor, Brewer, and Orono had grown, and the growth had begun to reach further and further out. It was in one of these towns that Reb and her husband made their home during a time before it became almost a suburb of the city. However, it was still a small town and was a place that Reb both loved and felt safe.

*　　*　　*

No matter where you went in Maine, there was one thing that like its neighboring New England states had and unlike the warmer climates, four very distinct seasons. Everyone had their favorite and not always what some would think were the obvious ones. Reb herself, when going through the years of menopause, actually loved winter the most because she could step outside the door and be in instant air-conditioning. She had friends who loved to ski, ice skate, snowmobile, and ice fish. For them, winter was the best time of year. There were times when winter was truly a spectacular scene to behold, after an ice storm with a blinding sun reflecting off icicle-laden trees or a fresh snowstorm that blanketed the fields before the sand or the salt from plows, human machinery or feet could mar it.

Reb knew others who were snowbirds and left for a warmer climate by November only to return in May. Still others loved the heat and lived for the days when they could bake in the sun and relish in the heat and humidity that July and August could and often did inevitably bring.

For Reb, her favorite season was spring which in Maine was always short. While Connecticut, New Hampshire, Massachusetts, and even southern Maine were often bathing in the renewal of springtime by the end of March and into April, the part of Maine that Reb lived in lived through a very cold, wet, muddy, and pretty dismal early spring complete with spring snow and ice storms. The leaves on the trees in her area did not return until the middle of May. Yet once the buds on the trees came out, the daffodils bloomed, and the grass turned green; spring was glorious in her part of Maine. Reb's favorite color was green with her favorite shade the pale color of early spring. Springtime for Reb lasted no longer than three weeks to a month followed sharply by the heat of summer, yet during that short time, Reb loved the color of the new leaves on the trees, the daffodils, the tulips, the apple and cherry blossoms, the early rhododendrons, even the early dandelions. Most of all, she loved the lilacs. They were her favorite flower, and she had a lot of them, more than anyone for miles around. Her lilacs had come with her property, and she was from time to time adding more. They were huge and old, much older than she was and probably as old as her house. This was a busy time of year. Getting the garden ready, shopping for the annuals to plant, planting the garden, simply being excited about another year. For Reb, the new year really began here, not on January 1.

Reb's next favorite season was fall. For her, at least, fall was the most beautiful time of all to be in Maine. At the peak of colors, Maine was a breathtaking place to be. The weather at this time of year was as perfect as perfect could be, warm in the day and cool at night, rarely humid or sticky, clear and easy to breathe. The black fly season of late spring and early summer was long gone. The mosquitoes were finding it a little too cold to stick around. The bees, the wasps, the earwigs, and all their other creepy little cousins were still around but sleepy and less in number. It was a new school year with the excitement of the little ones who were still young enough to be awed and with the excitement of their parents who were returning them. The apples were harvested as were the pumpkins. Potatoes, carrots, and turnips were dug up and placed in dry bins in cool places. Asters bloomed and potted mums stood on porches in bright fall colors. It was the colors, the changes in the foliage, nature's way of not allowing God's maples, birches, poplars and oaks to bear a weight that would break them that made this season special. This was the true beauty of fall in Maine, a season that couldn't be duplicated by the places in this world that were always warm.

Summer. Well, summer was the favorite season of many, if not most of the people Reb knew. It just wasn't hers.

Summer in Maine was beautiful. It was warm, often hot and always with warm nights. Reb did love the foliage of summer, the deep green of the leaves, and the lushness of the grass. She loved the brief and ever unfolding of the flowers from irises to roses to daisies, her red peonies, Johnny jump ups, and yellow lilies; the annuals that thrived in the summer, the pansies, the petunias and marigolds; the flowers planted by seed, zinnias and cosmos; and the many flowers that didn't come up, the one's that she kept trying to raise but just couldn't seem to get the knack of, the lupine, morning glories and sweet peas. Like everyone else, Reb loved being able to leave the house without a jacket, never take the time to warm up the car and be able to go anyplace without thinking about the weather. Like many people, Reb loved being outside, and in Maine, summer was the time to do it.

Yet, Reb hated heat and humidity. Not only did it make her uncomfortable, it made her sick. As the summer wore on, Reb's love of her garden and flowers would inevitably be replaced by a loathing for the amount of work it took to weed and water. Her hatred of the heat and humidity kept her in by day and only out during the coolest hours of the evening when there was still light. At least in the wintertime, Reb's air-conditioning was cheap, in fact, free. She only had to step outside the door. In the summertime, the air-conditioning ran long and was expensive and, in time, her garden and flowers would inevitably be overcome by the weeds.

Yes, Reb was a Maine girl. She had been to other places, and she had loved them. She would go back to Bermuda or Key West in a heartbeat. Yet in Maine, there was no other, no place, not one in the world, nothing like this place that bordered a country, an ocean and only one other state, a place rich in geography, seasons and people, the place of her family's history, her birth, her upbringing, and ultimately her nightmare, the memories of which would last a lifetime.

*   *   *

Reb's father was the first born son who never knew his mother and who was brought up by a father and stepmother who did not welcome his presence. His own mother, Victoria, had given birth to her first child, a daughter, at the age of seventeen. Reb's father was born two years later when his mother was nineteen. In later years, her father would be told that his mother had died giving birth to him, a story told to him in a way that gave him the message that he was to blame. In truth, his mother had died a year after that while giving birth to a third child, a son, who also died with his mother. From this point on, things were fuzzy and difficult for Reb to piece together.

*   *   *

Reb was often told that she looked like the Stines, her grandmother, Victoria's, family. Reb could never grasp this comparison because she had never seen pictures and had no way of knowing. From Reb's viewpoint, it was her sister that most resembled her father's side of the family. To Reb, she looked like her mother, at least in size and face.

*   *   *

After his mother's death, Julie, the first born and sister to her father, was shipped off to his mother's family to be raised, never to be seen again by her own father and, in fact, totally shunned. For whatever reason, Reb's father remained with his father, Albion, and eventually with a stepmother and a number of half brothers and sisters.

Reb's father's early years were difficult and full of many forms of abuse and neglect. His stepmother, Charlotte, must have felt threatened by his presence because her treatment of him or any other explanation of her treatment and behavior only painted her as being truly evil. Charlotte did everything possible to clearly communicate that Reb's father was not a welcome part of the family. He was ignored. He was sometimes beaten. He was often not fed and always poorly clothed. His bedroom was most often in the barn, and his closest companions were the cows and the goats. His father, Albion, was no better and certainly not caring or protective of his eldest son. In fact, he seemed determined to shun Reb's father just as he had done to his first-born daughter. It was a miracle that Reb's father could ever learn to love.

Reb's father's one saving grace was his relationship with his own grandfather, a gruff man by the name of Robert who in reality detested his own son and his son's treatment of his first born grandson. Yet Robert was a man of limited means and could not take on the role of raising Reb's father. He did, however, take his grandson whenever he could and gave him respite and a sense of belonging. So did his grandmothers, first Valentina, then Catherine.

Robert's first wife and the mother of Albion, Reb's grandfather, was a lady named Valentina, born on Valentine's Day in the early 1880s. One of Reb's most prized possessions were the actual valentines given by Robert to Valentina just before the turn of the twentieth century when they were what was in those days was called courting. Reb's father described Valentina as a tiny little lady who ran the house and brooked no argument yet put up with a lot of crap from his gruff and blustering grandfather. Even with the blustering and gruffness of her husband, Valentina was totally respected and somewhat feared by all, including Robert. She was also the person who introduced Reb's father to the world of Christianity and probably was one of the first people to show him that he was worthy of being loved. Unfortunately, she died sometime in early middle age. No one in Reb's family, including her mother, ever knew her, and Reb had never seen a picture. She had only the valentines.

After the death of his first wife, Robert met and married Catherine. Reb knew nothing more than that. She didn't know how old her great-grandmother Valentina had been when she died, and she didn't know just when and how Catherine and Robert got together. She did, however, have memories of her great Grammie Catherine, a tiny, sweet, soft-spoken woman with stark white hair, always coiffed in an elegant bun, cat's-eyed glasses and always dressed as though she were going to church complete with lace-collared dress and pearls. Grammie Catherine was a lady who lavished quiet love on her stepson's children. It was through Grammie Catherine that Reb had acquired her treasured valentines. Reb adored her great-grandmother and deeply mourned her death when it happened in the late 1960s. It was the first time that she was ever affected by death in a way that made her sad. Great Grampie Robert had died a couple of years before, but in Reb's young mind, her great-grandfather had been intimidating and just a little bit scary. To this seven-year-old, his death just meant that he wasn't there anymore and that she didn't have to avoid him.

It would be years before Reb would learn that her precious and beloved Grammie Catherine wasn't a blood relative. Reb's father had never treated Catherine as anything but a very special and treasured part of the family, and she was.

*   *   *

Robert and Catherine were the only true connections that her father and his children really had to that side of his family. With them gone, so was any lasting connection with her father's family. Robert, Valentina, and Catherine were perhaps the reason why Reb's father, even after all the abuse at the hand of his father and stepmother, still had the capacity to love.

*   *   *

Many, many years later, when Reb's father tried again to become part of the family that he was born into, neither he nor his wife and children would ever be recognized or considered part of the family. In future family reunions, Reb's entire family would attend but be treated as outsiders, not welcome, and certainly not part of Albion's family. The family that had given Reb her last name was a strange bunch, cold and distant. Reb would come to wonder if perhaps there was something with a touch of evil in her father's family, a touch of evil that one of her father's own would inherit.

*　　*　　*

In time, Reb's father would overcome much of the pain and neglect of his childhood. In time, he would be a success, at least compared to how his life began and certainly despite it.

*　　*　　*

Reb's father was also a good student who earned good marks in school. Once graduating from high school at the age of eighteen, he immediately enlisted in the navy and left his childhood home, never to return.

At fifteen, he had met Reb's mother, a beautiful brunette, at the weekly Grange Hall dance and was immediately smitten. Apparently, the attraction was mutual. For the next three years, they would meet at least once a week on Saturday night at the Grange Hall dance. By both of Reb's parents' account, they truly had eyes only for each other. In their 80s, they could still giggle about how they would wait for a break in the dance, sneak away from her grandmother's eagle eye and go outside to do a little necking. For both of her parents, there was never anyone else.

*   *   *

Reb's mother was raised in a strict Baptist home by a strong-minded working mother and a father who knew his place in the home and stayed in it. In old-fashioned terms, it would be called henpecked. Reb's grandmother was a very strong and well-educated woman who was years ahead of her time, strict and rigid in her expectations, strict in her religion and definitely head of the household.

Reb's mother was a natural beauty, small and petite, brunette with natural wavy hair, bright green eyes, a beautiful face, and a perfect body. She was quiet and sweet, dutiful and obedient, yet also had an independent and stubborn side that she did not show her mother. Reb's father had often told Reb that her mother as a young girl really was sweet and meek much of the time but stubborn and relentless when she felt she was right. In the end, it seemed that it was much more than her mother's beauty that her father had fallen in love with. It was also the sweetness and gentleness mixed with a measure of spark, sneakiness and determination.

Reb's mother was also the middle child. As a child, Reb's memories and perceptions of her mother were as a somewhat insecure person who needed her world to be a certain way and was weak in dealing with difficulties. The adult Reb often wondered if some of that was from being raised in a home as the middle child under the rule of a very domineering mother. As an older adult, Reb knew her mother well and understood that she was really a mixture of all those things—meek and insecure when scared, sweet and caring to those she loved, a tiger and determined when she felt she needed to be, much like Reb herself but for different reasons.

*   *   *

In November of 1949, Reb's dad returned long enough to marry his bride and take her back with him to his first port of call. In actuality, once enlisting in the navy, he had hitchhiked home as often as he could to visit. By the fall of 1949, he had presented her with a small diamond. After that, it was up to Reb's mother to decide when and how they would marry, and she did, in a small ceremony officiated by the church pastor with only her mother's older sister and brother-in-law in attendance. From there, they took off for Canada to honeymoon and began to build their life.

By this time, Reb's father had gone through submarine training and was shipped off to his first port of call in Norfolk, Virginia. Her parents bought their first trailer and lived on base, next traveling to Key West. Her dad was often out at sea, her mother keeping the small trailer ready for his on-shore time and herself working at the base bakery to bring in a little extra income. They were young, poor and free. These were some of the best times of their lives, and for Reb's father, this was the beginning of the family that he never had.

Over the next few years, Reb's dad would continue serving in the navy, serve through the Korean Conflict and for a few years after. Her parents would travel from Norfolk, Virginia, to Florida, leave Florida, travel to New Hampshire and Maine, and live in a variety of places. During the years between 1952 and 1958, four children would be born. Reb's oldest brother, born in 1952, would die three days after birth. After that, her parents would have three more children, a girl and two boys. In 1958, Reb's dad would leave the navy and return to Maine with his family. In the ensuing years, he would work at various jobs that would use his excellent mechanical and engineering skills. Reb would not be born until 1960, and by that time, the family would be living in their first house. This first house was painstakingly purchased by Reb's father and mother. It was her parents' start to the future that they both had long ago decided they would build together. It was also the place that would be the source of nightmares for three of their four children with one of their children being the source.

*   *   *

Not only was Reb the fourth and youngest child, but she was also the smallest, by far the smallest. From the beginning of her life, being born prematurely at less than six pounds, she was tiny and frail. She was always on the small side, thin and bony. She would spend all her growing years being told in one fashion or another how skinny, bony, and weak she was, sometimes with concern but more often with malice. Having to wear her cousin's large hand-me-downs; growing up and having very thin, fine, and unruly hair did nothing but confirm these observations for her. She was an ugly child, and she knew it.

Reb had two brothers and one sister, all older; two of them wonderful, one not.

* * *

It was September of 2011, and Reb had been through more than her share of tough times. At this point in her life, she is feeling desperate, terribly, terribly desperate, frightened, sadder, and more depressed than she has ever felt. That song, just the first few words, keeps running through her mind no matter where she is or what she is doing.

Reb is driving down the road, thinking, "If I could turn back time and do it all over again, if I could erase it all and do it all over again, what would I do? I'd like to have the chance. But, what would I do? I would go back and change so many things, so many wrong choices. I wouldn't do so many, many of the wrong things that I did. I'd go back in time knowing what I know today. I'd avoid the mistakes I've made. I would know what was to come. I would understand what would happen to me if I did certain things. I would be wiser. I would be the person I always thought I would be, the one I should be. Most of all, I wouldn't let it happen. Somehow, I wouldn't let it happen. The first me was the wrong one. The second me would be different."

"A problem. How far do I need to go back?" At first, she thought, back to the age of twelve. That was the year I started smoking." There were many reasons Reb started smoking at such a young age. First of all, her parents were both smokers. Her sister was a smoker; so were her brothers. Reb just didn't know it at the time. It was also the early 70s and a time when smoking was a natural and accepted part of society. It wasn't considered dirty, and it hadn't long been depicted as something that was addictive and bad for your health. In those days, smoking was something that was desired by many and for a kid like Reb who just wanted to belong; it was a rite of passage. The problem was that Reb and people like her really didn't have any idea of the danger. For Reb, it would be particularly detrimental because she was one of those people who would become heavily addicted. Her mother, father, sister, and one of her brothers would eventually give up the habit and never go back. Reb was never able to do it.

So for Reb, knowing what a horrible addiction it can be, going back, knowing what smoking really does, how it takes your health, wrinkles your skin, stains your clothes, your teeth, your walls, your windows, your everything it touches; how any smoker is now considered dirty and stupid and criminal in the eyes of a nonsmoking society, it would be a great start for a "do over." "Yes, back to a time before I smoked, one of the biggest mistakes I ever made."

Reb thought about it. "Yes, it would be great not to smoke, but would it be enough?" No. It wouldn't be enough. It wasn't enough. There was more that needed to be removed. "Okay, so I need to go back further."

"Okay," Reb thought. "What makes sense? What needs to go before the time when I started smoking?"

Reb wanted to sit on the thoughts and memories that she knew would be coming. She hated it; part of a truth when buried allowed her to live her life and do what needed to be done, the part of her life that had been so hard later for her family to hear, the part that some didn't believe or didn't want to believe, and a truth that would polarize a family, yet something else for Reb to feel guilty for.

A psychologist had once said she had PTSD. Reb knew this to be true, accepted it, and dealt with it, or so she thought. She had gone through the stages of shock, disbelief, rage, acceptance, and learning to live with it. She had tried therapy but ended up being her own best therapist. She had taught herself not to let these events, these memories rule her life. She would no longer give it the attention it didn't deserve. She needed the energy for other things, more important things, and her life was just too short to let him take any more from her. He had already taken her childhood. He wasn't going to get any more.

"A 'do over.' Never smoking is a start but not good enough. I have to go back further. I don't want to go there, but I have to. I can do this. I could go back and make it not happen," Reb thought about it. Detached, her objective self could do this.

*   *   *

Back to the year 1969. Reb was eight years old. She lived in an apartment in a house, the first house that her parents owned. It was a large gray slate house with three apartments, a small city-sized backyard and was the first real estate that her parents could afford to buy, the kind of house that needed a lot of work, the kind of house that still stands and still needs a lot of work. The apartment that Reb's family lived in had three floors. The first floor had only the kitchen and living room. The second floor had the bathroom and two bedrooms. One bedroom was for Reb's parents. The other bedroom was the largest and housed Reb and her brother, her youngest brother. In this room were a bunk bed, dressers, and toys, lots of toys. Reb's brother was the youngest of her two brothers, but he was older than she. On the third floor was a small landing and two more bedrooms; these were small with slanted ceilings. One was for Reb's sister, the oldest of the siblings, and the other one was for her other brother, her oldest brother.

Reb's sister was seven years older than she was. For sisters, this was a generation. Reb's earliest memories of her sister were of a tall girl with long, thick wavy brown hair, the hazel eyes of her mother and a sturdy build and form that had already passed girlhood. The bone structure of her face resembled Reb's father, long with a strong jaw and high cheek bones. Her sister was a pretty girl who would turn into a real beauty in her teens and early adulthood. Growing up, Reb looked up to, admired, and was often envious of her sister. As adults, their relationship would grow and change, and they would become the very best of friends and the closest of sisters. Growing up, however, the difference in their ages really was a generation. It would be a very long time before they would each understand and appreciate just what the nightmare in their home had done to them. There was much that Reb didn't know about her sister, and there was much that her sister didn't know about her.

Reb's youngest brother was only two years older than she was. Like her, he was of short stature and small of build, just not skinny and bony like Reb was. Like her, he resembled his mother in most ways from the hazel-green eyes to the wide nose and round face that didn't have the strong prominent jaw and high cheek bones of her father and sister but still had an appeal all its own. In reality, Sammy was just plain cute. There was no other word for it. He had a look, a smile and a way about him that endeared him to most. In appearance, there was no doubt that Reb and Sammy were siblings. She just didn't have the same qualities that made her brother so endearing.

Reb's oldest brother was a different story. In physical appearance, he bore the strongest resemblance to Reb's father. He was the only one with her father's blue eyes and the only right-handed child in the family. Reb's oldest brother, older by five years, was much bigger and stronger than she was, bigger by ninety pounds and taller by a foot.

Reb's oldest brother was a bully and had always been a bully. He was aggressive. He was the consummate liar. He was determined, and he was smart. He was also jealous. He was jealous of anyone and anything that took attention away from him. He wanted what he wanted and would do anything to get it. For Reb, her sister, and Sammy, they could and would never form any affection for this brother because they were always afraid of him.

Reb's oldest brother was jealous, jealous of her oldest sister, jealous of Sammy, and most of all, jealous of Reb. She was a little girl, very much loved by her mother and protected, at least so he thought. He had had much practice in bullying, and he had been successful in the neighborhood, at school, and at home.

Reb's oldest brother loved to practice his aggression on her, but she wasn't the only one. He terrorized many a smaller boy in the neighborhood and school. He terrorized his younger brother. He had terrorized his older sister as well.

*   *   *

For a very long time, Reb had been under the impression that her sister had received the lightest dose of the abuse. She had been wrong. The truth was that this brother had started his litany of terror long before Reb was born, from the time he was able to walk and show whatever strength and muscle he had. Reb's sister remembered time upon time when she was hit, kicked, and beaten on by Billy, even a time when Billy had wanted her off the swing she was on, threw a large rock at her head and split her head wide open. The protection for Sissy had been as little or as ineffective as it would be for Sammy and for Reb. In time, through the combination of her father's corporal punishment and Sissy's own strength, Billy would eventually learn that his older sister was not an easy target, and for her, the beatings stopped. The memories and the terror she had felt never would.

If ultimately he couldn't control his older sister, Billy was successful in bullying his mother. He had first put terror in his mother's heart when at the age of three, he threatened and chased her with a knife. Reb's dad worked two jobs and wasn't home very often. Billy's best bet, however, would turn out to be Reb.

*   *   *

If this had happened in 2011, Reb's oldest brother would have been removed from the home somehow. There would have been someone who would have recognized the signs and made the appropriate report to the appropriate agency, and he would have been removed. If not taken out of the home, the rest of the kids would have been removed and protected. But this wasn't 2011. It wasn't during the 2000s, the 1990s, or the 1980s when Reb was teaching. It was the 1960s, and this type of thing wasn't talked about, much less really dealt with unless it was blatant, but the problems in Reb's home were kept quiet. No one, not the teachers, not the relatives, not the neighbors, no one knew. It just was what it was, and it was Reb's job to survive.

Even in the 1960s, the word *abuse* was used and understood, but the label didn't exist for Reb at that time, and she had no idea.

*   *   *

Reb thought, "I need to go back further. But how far? When did the abuse start?"

The beginnings of it were fuzzy. She really couldn't remember exactly when the beatings started. Reb had worked so hard to squash the memories. She supposed that they had to have started when she was very young, something like four. She couldn't remember a time in her childhood when her oldest brother wasn't beating on her, finding ways to humiliate her, threatening her. She may have been terrified at the time, but she just couldn't remember. It had happened so often that many of the actual events became blurred. It was just something that was part of her life, something that she didn't even know shouldn't be happening, something she endured and survived but never told.

She was trying to be a good girl. He kept telling her that if she told, he would kill her. She believed him, and she was trying to survive.

If only it hadn't been so much worse than the beatings.

So when should the "do over" begin? Certainly, before she was eight.

*   *   *

On a certain night in 1968 or 1969 when she was eight years old, Reb couldn't remember the exact date, her oldest brother asked her to come up to his room. He wanted to talk to her. When he was in one of his friendly moods, he would often come to her room and play with her toys, especially her Barbie dolls, and would often bring in his own GI Joe. On this night, Reb's oldest brother asked her to bring some of her Barbie dolls upstairs to his room. Reb did. Reb's oldest brother had always been fascinated by her Barbie dolls, and she had a great collection. Reb had no way of knowing or understanding this, but her oldest brother also had a fascination with woman's bodies. Reb's Barbie dolls were in perfect condition.

On that certain night in 1968 or 1969, Reb did as she was asked and brought the case containing her Barbies upstairs to her brother's room. Once the door was closed, oldest brother helped Reb take the Barbies out of the case. Oldest brother undressed them. He remarked at the perfect body of the Barbies and ran his fingers over them. Oldest brother then explained why. He told Reb that he could show her how to be a woman like the Barbies. He explained that he could show how Reb could be a woman and a mother like Mom. He could teach her how to be like Mom.

Older brother then undressed Reb and took her to his bed. He kissed her and told her how someday she would look like the Barbie. He told her again that he could show her what it meant to be a woman, to be a mother. He tried. He really tried, but then, just then, Reb got scared. It was odd and scary, and it didn't feel right. She just knew that it wasn't right. She found a way to get up, get dressed, and she went downstairs to her own bedroom.

*   *   *

Reb's parents may not have been home that night, or at least she didn't remember them being home that night. Her father might have been working; her mother might have been sleeping or watching TV. She couldn't remember where her sister or other brother had been. They all could have been nearby. Maybe her oldest brother was babysitting. In truth, she couldn't remember, but that night, she knew that something very bad had happened to her. She was confused and scared.

* * *

Oldest brother soon found her and threatened her. If Reb ever told, he would kill her, and he had proven that he could do it. Reb had seen. Reb had experienced the beatings. She still felt the pain, and she knew it to be true. She never told, not for many, many years.

* * *

For many years, Reb buried this memory, this event and tried to act as though it had never happened. Even as a little girl, Reb had figured certain things out and knew that her mother could never handle the truth. Her mother got upset very easily, and Reb felt a strong protective instinct. She was too young to realize that the roles had been reversed. Reb never told anyone until she was seventeen years old, and the person she told would be of little consequence in her adult life.

She finally told her parents, her sister, and other brother when she was twenty-six years old. She told because she could no longer pretend. She had had an altercation with her oldest brother that had threatened someone she loved more than anything in the world, her son. She could no longer pretend for the sake of keeping the family together, so she told, but most didn't believe her.

* * *

"Now," Reb thought, "I could go back to the age of seven and not let it happen. I would know what sex and abuse and incest is. I would not go in that room. If he came near me, I would scream to the top of my lungs. I would tell my mother. I would tell my father. I would tell and tell and tell, and it would never happen."

What a difference that one change would make. It would take away so many nightmares, so many fears that Reb had so long since buried. But would it be enough? Could it be enough? No, it wouldn't. It just wouldn't. There was still one more thing, the worst of all.

* * *

In January of 1999, Reb was thirty-eight years old. She had been suffering from severe menstrual problems for many, many years. That month, she had a total hysterectomy. It took her many months to recuperate from the operation, but it was worth it. The operation improved so many problems. It created others, one which was incredible, unbelievable, and totally unexpected.

Reb's body changed after the hysterectomy. She gained weight and was stronger. She gained so much weight that she had to go out and buy a whole new wardrobe, which she loved. She had her engagement and wedding rings resized. For the first time in her life, her bones did not show through her limbs. For the first time, she was a normal size. She had energy. The black moods were gone. The bloating was gone. The horrible periods were gone. Reb was ecstatic.

Of course, there were trade-offs. The operation sent her straight into menopause. The hot flashes were awful, but she could take medicine for that. Things were definitely better, or so she thought.

Sometime in April of that same year, Reb's legs began to ache, really ache. She started having problems walking. She couldn't walk for long without needing to rest and with each day became more and more exhausted with the effort. One day while at work, Reb was standing at the photo copier printing off reports she had written when she fell to the floor. She just went down. No warning. No apparent reason. She just fell to the floor and could not move her legs. When she was able to get up, the aching was greater than ever. Within days, she would be walking with a cane.

*   *   *

Reb hated to go to the doctor's. She had an innate distrust and fear of the whole medical profession. In her experience, most of the medical treatment she had had consisted of tests that were painful and cures that were often worse than the original problem. Most of all, Reb had a firm belief that most of these people saw only the physical yet never cared at all for the person. Reb knew that a doctor might see her viewpoint as ridiculous. After all, it was the job of the medical professionals to identify and treat. Yet to Reb, the clinical and sometimes even superior attitude and mannerisms of many doctors she had encountered over the years was intimidating to her and therefore something to be avoided. In Reb's early days of teaching, she had been taught and learned to live by a very basic philosophy. People don't care how much you know until they know how much you care. In Reb's opinion, most doctors cared more about their station in life and the money and prestige it earned them, not the patients that they served.

Reb's doctor was different, and Reb trusted her. She had been going to this one doctor for a long time; they had a good relationship, and the pain was horrible. She could hardly walk, so back to her doctor she went. Reb's doctor ordered a series of tests, including a bone scan and x-rays.

A few days after the tests were completed, Reb received a call at work. It was from a nurse at her doctor's office. "We have your test results, and Dr. Smith would like you to come in. The scan showed that you have two broken legs, well, really fractures, old injuries that didn't heal properly."

Reb was shocked and asked for the information to be repeated so that she was sure that she had heard correctly. She had. "No way, my legs aren't broken! I think I would know if my legs were broken!"

"Your pelvis is fractured as well. They are old injuries that didn't heal properly. The x-rays showed broken ribs as well. Dr. Smith will discuss more about this when she sees you. You need to come in soon."

Reb didn't believe it. She just couldn't understand. Her legs were not fractured! Her pelvis was not fractured! She had known about the broken ribs from a previous x-ray in her teens, and she knew how that had happened. She just hadn't told her doctor. What the hell!

When Reb went back to her doctor, it was explained to her that there were old, once-healed fractures of both upper thighs, her pelvis, and two broken ribs. Apparently, when she had the hysterectomy, the resulting changes in her body had allowed the fractures to open, and severe arthritis formed in all the areas of the original injury.

*   *   *

Reb thought back to when her son was born. He had been overdue by a month, and Reb had had a planned C-section. During the months she was pregnant, she had utilized the services of a midwife and had never been examined by the obstetrician but because she was so late in going into labor, a C-section was planned with a final check from the obstetrician the day before her son was born. Upon doing the pelvic examination, the obstetrician made a very odd statement with an even odder conclusion. "Well, no wonder. There is no way she can have this baby. She never would have gone into labor." At the time, Reb was very young, confused, tired, large, uncomfortable, totally miserable, and alone. She just wanted to have the baby. She didn't care why she couldn't go into labor and didn't ask any questions. She should have.

*   *   *

When her doctor explained all the old injuries, Reb knew that the fracture of her pelvis had to be the reason why she never went into labor in 1984 when she gave birth to her son. She just didn't want to believe how it had happened. Reb had buried her childhood so deeply that she didn't want to even entertain the thought. The problem was, she had to.

Dr. Smith asked Reb, "The fractures are old. They are childhood injuries. Do you remember fracturing your legs? What happened to cause this?"

Reb had never knowingly fractured her thighs, her pelvis, or her ribs. She had broken her right arm when she was four and remembered that well. She had fallen off a bike and had her arm in a cast and sling for months. But she didn't remember ever knowingly breaking a leg, much less both legs. As a child, she didn't even know what a pelvis was, and she certainly didn't know she had fractured it. Reb knew about the two broken ribs, and she knew how that had happened.

*   *   *

When Reb was a child, she was often in pain. Pain was a normal part of her life, something she thought everyone else had as well. The worst pain were the migraines that aspirin only made worse, and only her dad's rocking her and sleep would make feel better. The migraines often made the pain in her legs seem mild in comparison.

Reb was never strong. She had no muscles that showed. She was always the smallest, the skinniest, and the weakest. She never got into sports and, in fact, wasn't good at most of them. She liked to swim and loved to play catch. She also loved to run, and when she ran, she could run really fast. She even beat the fastest boy in elementary school. The problem was it hurt to run, and as she got older, running became more and more difficult. The pain in her legs made her more and more accident prone, and as she got older, it just got harder. By the time she went to college, she avoided running completely.

*   *   *

Dr. Smith was baffled. She asked Reb, "Do you remember anything that could have happened? Your injuries are old. They had to have happened a long time ago." Reb thought about it, although she really didn't need to think about it for long. She just didn't want to go there.

"Could something that happened when I was a child be the reason?" Dr. Smith had known Reb for a long time and this had never come up. Reb had never said anything about her childhood. Dr. Smith waited for Reb to explain.

*   *   *

Between the time from 1964 when Reb was four, at the earliest time she could remember, and 1975 when Reb was fourteen, Reb was regularly bullied and beaten by her oldest brother. Sometimes, the beatings were with fists to the ribs, stomach, and legs; never to the face and never in a place that showed. Sometimes, she would be thrown into bushes, on the ground or down entire flights of stairs. Sometimes, it was just verbal, calling her names, spreading rumors. Sometimes, it was throwing things at her. The only predictability was that it would almost always happen when her parents weren't watching, and always, always, she would be warned that if she told, he would kill her. She had no reason not to believe him. The number of and the level of violence in the beatings became much worse after the night in his bedroom with the Barbie dolls.

*   *   *

Reb went on to explain, "I have a brother who beat me when I was a child. He was really mean. He hit me a lot and threw me down the stairs. He did it for a long time. Once, when I was eight, he tried to do something sexual with me." Reb couldn't bring herself to use the term incest. "Could that be it?"

Dr. Smith stopped in her tracks. She was stunned. She knew her patient and knew that she was being honest, but it wasn't often that something like this happened in her practice. How to respond? She knew this patient and would have to take things carefully. "Yes. It could have happened this way. You were never in an accident? Any kind of accident?"

"No. Never."

*   *   *

No. Reb had never been in any kind of accident. She had broken her arm when she was four when she fell off a bike, so maybe that would be considered an accident. But she had never been in a car accident, a household accident, or any kind of accident that would account for the injuries that the doctor was telling her she had.

She remembered when her ribs were broken. It was during a particularly bad beating her oldest brother had given her, one where his temper really got the better of him, and he punched her hard in the ribs. She had hurt for months after. Years later, Reb had an x-ray of the area because of a lump found on her breast. The lump turned out to be a normal mass of tissue. The x-ray had shown two ribs that had healed but were distorted, as if they had never been treated.

The poorly healed rib fractures had been surprising to her doctor but not to Reb. She remembered the incident and the pain, and she knew why it had happened. Even then, though, she didn't tell the doctor when or how it had happened. It was part of the never telling that was so engrained in her. But, it was also the beginning of her anger, an anger that she had worked hard to suppress.

*   *   *

"I think that what happened to you probably happened in childhood. I think that it did happen when you were a child. It all fits. I'm sorry that this happened to you." Now Reb was the one who was stunned. She could only reply, "This is going to hurt my family. Are you sure that this is it? I don't want to hurt my family. My husband will be horrified."

Dr. Smith was a rare doctor, one with compassion. Her mind did not immediately leap to the thought of how could a person allow this to happen to herself. She was amazed that this woman who had just figured out that her past was the reason for her condition, that this woman, who had endured such horror, was more concerned about her family than for herself, but she also understood that this was part of the problem, that it was going to be a difficult journey for her patient. She couldn't help but remark to Reb that she was surprised at the compassion given what she had been through and what was now before her. But, Reb couldn't register her doctor's words. She was again on shut down and simply couldn't deal with anymore. She accepted her doctor's prescription for Vioxx and went home. She would see her doctor again soon.

*   *   *

When Reb got home that afternoon, her mind simply couldn't and wouldn't process all that had happened. She went through the motions of making dinner, doing chores and polite conversation. She couldn't talk about it.

Her husband recognized the signs and didn't push. He knew about the test results because Reb had told him about it the day before. He also knew about what her oldest brother had done to her. He was one of the only people Reb had ever confided in. He just had no idea that the two were connected. Oh, the things he would like to do to the rotten bastard.

*　　*　　*

Reb was strong in many ways. She was intelligent and creative. She wasn't creative artistically. That was a blessing given to her sister and youngest brother, not to her. But she was creative in solving problems. She also had an instinct about people and usually read them accurately. She would watch and listen to everything and everyone around her. She could move through a problem and find ways to resolve them in ways that no one else considered. She could always see in her mind what the end product of any situation should be, whether it be in teaching a child to speak or making decisions regarding the larger picture of a student's total education. She could break things down and in her mind see the steps that would need to be taken in order to move forward. Solving the problem was always her goal and was one of the things that made her particularly good at her job in her many roles as a therapist, teacher, and administrator. She was a great teacher because she instinctively understood how to teach, how to motivate, and most importantly, she understood that caring was the most important thing.

Reb was not so bright as to be the intellectual type. She disliked and distrusted people who were so intellectually superior that they worshiped their own intellect and found themselves to be above others, always pushing that their point of view was the only point of view and being insulted when others didn't agree. It was one of the reasons why she so mistrusted doctors. There were too many in her experience who listened and trusted in their own intellect so much that they couldn't and wouldn't listen to their patients and were offended when someone suggested that there might be another way of looking at things.

Even more, she disliked bullies the most and could recognize one, adult or child, almost instantly. She was insecure about a lot of things and disliked confrontation, but when confronted with a bully or a situation she knew to be wrong, she was stubborn, reactive, and sometimes fearless. In her career, she had seen a lot and dealt with all kinds of people, wealthy people, politicians, lawyers, doctors, teachers, poor people, people on welfare, people with mental illness, and people who could cause mental illness just by the things they did to others. You name it, and she had probably dealt with it.

She had also dealt with children with a variety of problems, disabilities and challenges, some more successfully than others but always with the best of intentions. Reb had never dealt with anyone like her.

*   *   *

Reb's husband was wise at times. He recognized that there was something very, very wrong. He also knew that his wife would talk when she was ready to.

It took a few days before Reb was ready to talk to anyone. When she did, she confided to her husband. When she confided, she told him more than she had ever told him before. He had known that her oldest brother had been abusive. He could never have guessed that it was this bad. He was angry, very angry and couldn't understand how the son of a bitch had gotten away with it. He didn't understand how Reb could have let him get away with this. He wanted to kill the son of a bitch. Reb didn't want to admit it, but so did she.

*   *   *

As time went on, Reb went through things she couldn't prevent, things she had no control over. Almost immediately after finding out the truth, Reb began having nightmares, again. She had had lots of them when she was a child and in her early adulthood, but they had left her many years ago during all the years that she had been able to stuff the memories away, during all the years that she was building her life. Now, she dreamed every night, dreams of her brother raping her, dreams of her brother stabbing her, dreams of her screaming at her parents, dreams of them not believing her, dreams of her family rejecting her when she told the truth. During waking hours, she couldn't watch any TV that was violent in nature, particularly anything that involved children. She would shake and cry and couldn't control it. No one, not her husband, not her relatives, could do anything to help. For the rest of her life, whenever her brother's name was said or anything past or present related to him was discussed, she would have what she called the "Billy dreams." Knowing that these dreams would probably happen made her cringe every time her brother's name was mentioned, and it would be mentioned many times throughout the years.

As time went on in 1999, Reb became more and more despondent. At first, she was in a state of shock and disbelief. She couldn't deal with anything. She really, really tried, but she just couldn't help what was happening to her, something that she had always been able to do before. As the shock began to wear off, she became angry, really, really angry, furious.

*　　*　　*

In her childhood, she had never allowed herself to be angry. When she was young, she found that the best way to cope was to simply not allow herself to feel anger or any other emotion. In her young mind, being angry accomplished nothing. It got her nowhere, and she would never escape. Surviving and escaping was the only way. Moving forward was the only way. Her parents had taught her to be practical, and this was practical. Stuffing the emotions and being practical had also moved her through many things and forward to accomplishing goals and achievements she was proud of and had worked hard to achieve. It was part of what some people like her did to survive, something she would later understand would never be understood by those who were fortunate enough to be brought up in a world different from hers.

*　　*　　*

The young Reb had found a way to stuff most of the emotions, but the older Reb couldn't do it any longer. She was angry, very angry. She was pissed off. This Reb knew just how bad it really was; what had really happened to her. This Reb knew that life should have been different for her. This was anger and rage, feelings that she didn't like and didn't want to show. This was something that she couldn't control.

Uncontrollable anger wasn't good, and Reb didn't like it. It wasn't natural to the person who had for so long been able to keep it all just below the surface, the person that had only been able to move on by burying the truth.

This Reb was pissed off that she could no longer protect herself or the integrity of her family. She could no longer shield anyone else, not her mother, not her father, not her sister, not her other brother, not her husband, and not even her son.

Her legs were fractured. Her pelvis was fractured. Her ribs were broken. She had great trouble walking and was in constant pain. She was missing work more often than she should and when she did go to work, she walked with a cane. When she was at work, her peers asked her questions that she didn't want to answer. Even worse, her students asked her questions and being as young as they were, many were alarmed by her cane. The situation was terrible, and she had done nothing to cause it. It had been caused by someone else, and she could no longer control the rage that had been simmering under the surface.

*   *   *

In her role as a speech therapist, Reb traveled between schools most days and carried large amounts of materials and paperwork. In her role as a special education coordinator, she carried a laptop from school to school, scheduled and ran meetings, often functioned as an administrator, took the minutes of meetings, and spent most evenings and many overtime hours writing reports. In her role as a therapist, she worked with very young and active special needs children, some violent. She had always worked hard and had gained a great deal of proficiency and expertise over the years, but her job was very difficult and took a lot of energy, stamina, and strength. The job was difficult for a person in good health, but it was impossible for a woman with fractured legs, constant pain, and walking with a cane.

Reb was proud of the job she did. She worked really, really hard and was good at it. It was one of the few things in her life that she knew she did well. She cared deeply about the kids. She cared deeply about the teachers she worked with. She relished the challenge that many of the students presented. She understood the stress that the teachers faced every day because she lived it in triplicate. She tried to understand the parents of her students, although this was sometimes difficult.

Of course, there were parts of her job that she disliked, a few things that she really hated. She detested parents who used the system for their own platform. She detested parents who put their own needs before their children. She abhorred teachers who were absolutely rigid in their ways and couldn't change to meet a student's needs. She detested the same tendency in a few of the coworkers in her field. She learned to be wary of administrators who were out of touch, bullied,

A few years before 1999 when Reb was in her early thirties, she had come to a point in her life when she realized that she couldn't go it alone, that she needed more and that there was someone out there whom she needed to seek.

It began with a situation at work. At the time, Reb's special education director, Dr. Scott, was a small bully of a man who had yet to go through the personal crisis that would finally turn him into a human being. At the time, his main goal was in making the lives of the district's special education teachers and therapists miserable, often threatening that if they didn't like his rules, they were welcome to go elsewhere. Part of the rules was in enforcing certain criteria and rules for therapy services that did not meet the needs of the students but did keep the numbers down, a much desired end for both the city and the state budget. Within this climate, Reb had a special student, one whom she instinctively knew was not only being underserved but misdiagnosed. It was a little girl who had been labeled as mentally retarded, yet after working for months with the child, Reb was convinced that she wasn't. What she was was severely impaired in both her communication skills and in the home that she lived in, perhaps most of all because of the home she lived in. Underneath it all was a bright child who just might have a chance if she got the right kind of help, and Reb wanted to give that to her. The climate of the time, however, wouldn't allow it. It was simple. Services were based on the results of testing. If a student's verbal IQ was roughly equal to his or her tested abilities in oral language, the child was not to receive therapy services because, at least in those times, there was no gap, no potential for improvement. Thus, Dr. Scott ordered Reb not to see the student. When she tried valiantly to argue the point, she was very emphatically told that to see this student was a direct act of insubordination and that she would be fired.

In her heart, Reb couldn't understand and was angry, very angry. At the time, Reb was in her very early thirties, still not understanding that her fear of bullies like Dr. Scott was engrained in her down to her very soul but old enough to understand that what had been done to this student was wrong. Maybe it was the lack of communication skills and the home that this child lived in that connected Reb so strongly to this particular student. Maybe it was the fact that Reb could see what was possible for this little girl. In any case, Reb had no choice but to do as she was ordered and let it go.

This event brought on a wave of anger and negative emotions, mostly of living in a world that shut good people down from doing the right thing. In this, Reb turned to her best friend, Betty, who was also her sister-in-law. It was Betty that led Reb to the One who would give her the faith to endure.

• •

Reb's immediate family had either rejected or were lukewarm on the One she was seeking, and she had had little in the way of this as a child. Much of her larger family, many generations, in fact, had embraced Him, and He was a focal point in their lives. For many reasons, Reb was led to Him. Early in her thirties, Reb became a Christian.

* * *

Becoming a Christian was the best thing that ever happened to Reb. Knowing the Lord and being forgiven for her sins strengthened her in ways that no one could understand. In the early days of her being a born-again Christian, most of her family didn't understand and were suspicious of the changes in her. She could be overzealous and push her views on others when it wasn't welcome. Knowing what she knew and understanding what she did about God and where she would be going after she died made her push to have her loved ones certain of the same fate. Through the years, she would learn to temper this understanding knowing that if it were meant to be, God would work it out in his time and in his way.

Reb attended the family church, a little white country church complete with steeple and bell, a church that had been founded by one of her ancestors in the mid-1800s. In this place, she was surrounded by extended family members, aunts, uncles, and cousins who had long accepted the Lord as their savior and who gently guided her.

In this environment, her spirit flourished. During those years, Reb did many things that she never thought she could do. She had a pretty good voice and joined the choir, which she loved. She sang duets and solos and participated in many church performances. Sometimes, she was able to bring in friends, family, and in-law relatives to participate in holiday performances. Her parents started to go to church again, probably just to hear their daughter sing, but the point was that they came, and it became an important part of their lives as well.

Reb read. She read a lot. Her curiosity and need to learn was great, and she devoured most of the books in the church library. She read the Bible from cover to cover and then read it four more times. She went to Women's Bible classes, Christian conventions and adult Sunday School. Like many Christians, Reb eagerly waited for the next in the Left Behind series to come out and read eagerly all ranges of perspective on the end times. It was a time of growth, excitement, and peace.

Reb also taught Sunday school. She loved working with the younger children and volunteered to teach the preschoolers and kindergarten. She taught Junior Church and relished in creating lessons that would motivate and keep children coming back. She taught Vacation Bible School so well that she had more children than she could handle. She wrote one Christmas play and directed Christmas and Easter plays that filled every seat with the children's parents, relatives and friends. She put a lot of her own money into all these adventures. She loved every minute of it, every adult and every child. The greatest compliment she ever received was from the Sunday School superintendent who publicly said that she was "a natural and gifted teacher."

*   *   *

In 1999, Reb's health began to affect her responsibilities in church as well. It started with Sunday School. She was in too much pain and too tired to prepare the lessons and to deal with the young energetic preschoolers and kindergarteners, so she gave this up. Next was Junior Church, same reason, and that went too.

When plans were being made for Vacation Bible School, she bowed out. Reb left these responsibilities with a heavy heart and yet more anger.

The one thing that Reb was able to hold onto in 1999 and for a few years after was her place in the choir. This was a way to serve that didn't require the amount of preparation and energy that Reb could no longer do. It was also the avenue that led her for the first time to strike out at her parents.

*　　*　　*

As an adult, Reb had always been close to her parents, but there was a definite dividing line between her childhood years and her adulthood. Many of Reb's memories of childhood were blurred, squashed and avoided because of the abuse. There was little from her childhood that she wanted to remember, so she buried most of it. What she could remember was a father who worked all the time to provide and a mother who worked all the time at home to hold the home together.

Her mother was a beautiful woman. She really was. Reb had inherited her bright hazel eyes from her mother. Her mother was a small, petite woman with dark naturally wavy hair that she insisted on putting in rollers every day. In her prime, she was a true beauty, and she would look younger than her age until well into her sixties. In the early 1950s, when her parents were very young and her father was overseas, he had taken a snapshot of her mother and had a painting done in Paris. Reb now had the painting, and it hung in her house. It was one of her most prized possessions. Her mother had a beautiful face, and it was the one thing, besides her hazel eyes, that Reb had inherited. In this, Reb looked like her mother. She just didn't inherit the hair and the body to go along with it. Her sister did. Reb inherited her father's nearly jet black and very straight, fine and unruly hair. Reb's thin, frail and bony body was something that must have started with her. No one else in the family had it.

Reb's mother worked hard by day cleaning, doing laundry, and taking care of her children. Her mother was always there when Reb came home for lunch, and she was always there when Reb came home from school. Reb's mother was an earnest and loving person who needed to have her life played out in a certain way. Certain realities and problems couldn't be borne. They were too painful or too scary for her. Reb figured this out at a very early age and protected her mother. It was the first and most important reason why Reb never talked about the things that her oldest brother did.

While in curlers and housedress by day, Reb's mother showed her beauty by night. Each night when her father was home, once the dishes were done, her mother disappeared for a while and turned up later completely decked out. Whether it was just to sit near Reb's father and watch TV or talk over the day, her mother would look her best. Her hair would be perfectly coiffed. Her makeup was on, and she would be wearing her prettiest dress complete with clip-on pearl earrings, a pearl necklace and high heels. In later years, Reb would watch reruns of *the Donna Reed Show* and realize that that was the way her mother had been. Donna Reed's world had been perfect. Maybe that's what her mother had been trying to create.

Reb's mother grew up in a family of a mother, father and two sisters. She was the middle child. A large part of her nature was shy, quiet, and insecure, a person who was easily intimidated, especially by her mother. Reb's mother's family were staunch Baptists and she was brought up under the very strict rules of a Baptist home. Reb's grandmother was a strong and intelligent woman who in some ways defied the times by being a working mother. She had attended the Farmington Teacher's College in the early 1900s, had graduated, and had taught school in one-room school houses and small schools for a career that lasted more than forty years. Although Reb's grandfather also worked and had a long career in the railroad, it was her grandmother that was the head of the house. The three girls were taught to be obedient, get good marks in school, take care of the house, and do everything their mother told them to do. All three girls grew up to marry young, against their mother's wish in weddings that their mother did not attend.

*   *   *

Reb's father was a hardworking man who had come from a very painful and abusive upbringing. His mother had died when he was very young, and he had never known her. He was raised by his father and stepmother, a stepmother who felt threatened by his presence and did not want him around. His father was an ignorant, cruel man who preferred the children that his second wife bore him. He allowed his first wife's family to raise his first-born child, a daughter, and never had anything to do with her. He grudgingly tolerated the presence of his eldest son. He had a violent temper and often took his frustrations out on Reb's father. There were many times when Reb's father did not have a meal to eat or proper clothes to wear. In extreme irony, the stepmother was anything but faithful to Reb's grandfather and, in fact, engaged in an affair that produced a child of another race, a child that was accepted by the family while Reb's father was not.

Reb's parents were born during the depression and raised during those years and throughout the years of World War II. By today's standard, they were brought up in poverty. Reb's mother had a school dress, a day dress and a church dress. Reb's father had a set of overalls for work and a set of clothes for school. That was it, no choices. To go to school, there was no bus. They walked, biked or hitched. Food choices were whatever was served and in her father's case, sometimes not even that. Neither of them ever had running water. Both of them went to the outhouse. When hurt or distressed, there was no processing or talking it through with a caring adult, and little comforting. In her father's case, there was no one and nothing. But there was the constant lesson of hard work, a belief in certain truths and a desire to move forward. In her father's case, the abuse that he endured as a child and the desire to move forward led him to leave home the day after he graduated from high school and never look back. In her mother's case, she fell in love, married, and started a family as her way of getting out. Together, they worked hard and slowly, methodically built their future. Reb's parents were in many ways very smart and very wise people, but they were truly innocent in certain ways, extremely frugal in most ways, and totally blind in the ways that would damage their family the most.

*   *   *

Reb's sister was the exact opposite of her. Whereas Reb was extremely tiny, underweight, and frail, her sister was larger boned, taller, stronger and beautiful. Reb's sister was the oldest in the family, the strongest in spirit, and a true renegade. Reb called her "Sissy," and Sissy always knew best. Sissy was also the first to work hard at escaping a house that was impossible to live in, and she did it by any means possible, some right, some wrong, but she got away.

Reb's youngest brother was one of her best friends when she was growing up. He was smaller like her, gentle and caring in the ways that counted, wilder than hell in the ways that her parents rarely figured out, smart, talented, funny, motivated, and a total brat.

Reb adored both her sister and her youngest brother. They would all go in very different directions in adulthood but would become closer and closer as time went on.

*　　*　　*

Reb's oldest brother was much taller than she. He was taller than her youngest brother. He was taller than her sister. He was also much heavier and physically tougher than Reb and her youngest brother. Reb's oldest brother was big, mean, and nasty. He was smart and very cunning. He was jealous, selfish, and very intent on meeting his own ends, whatever it took. The big, mean, and nasty part of him led him to beat up Reb, her sister, her youngest brother, and many of the kids in the neighborhood. He had beaten on Reb's oldest sister but eventually got as good as he gave. However, it was the jealous part of his nature that made him do his worst to Reb's youngest brother and to her, and it was the selfish and truly evil part of his nature that he used on Reb. He used his cunning in the form of threatening to cover up whatever he did.

Reb would come to understand that this particular brother in truth had no conscience besides what was necessary to meet his own needs. Whether he inherited it from his father's father, some other descendant or was just born evil, Reb didn't know, but he was evil, and he would do nothing in his life that in her mind would ever prove otherwise.

Reb was afraid of her oldest brother, but most of all, she learned to hate him.

*   *   *

With such diversity in looks and personality, in their earliest years, Reb, her sister, and brothers grew up in a home that was impoverished yet still met the needs for survival. Her father worked at least two jobs at all times. Her mother worked hard to keep a very clean house, and she did. The house was always clean and neat, the beds made, everything scrubbed and shined. Her mother prepared and cooked all the meals including being understanding of fussy children, never forcing foods on her kids that they disliked. Her mother was always there when the kids came home from school.

For clothing, all four of the children were clothed but not well. While their parents spent their childhood clothed in three very specific outfits, one for home, one for school, and one for church, Reb and her siblings had more clothes, but they were in the form of hand-me-downs from the 1950s, ill-fitting, ridiculous clothing from relatives. It was a situation that all the children abhorred because they really looked like they were wearing hand-me-downs. Reb had it the worst because she was tiny and had a height and frame that was different from anyone else in her family, including relatives. As with her brothers and sister, she would look ridiculous until she was able to earn money and buy her own clothes. It was an issue that would create a problem for all four of the children in later years. They all developed a need for very large wardrobes in their adult years and would spend a lot of money on clothing.

For Reb, the issue with the hand-me-downs was particularly painful. She was the only child who was extremely thin, short, and homely. She was always shorter and much, much smaller than anyone in her class. She had crooked teeth and very thin, straight and short hair parted on the side in a very unflattering way. Her loose-fitting, out-of-style and ridiculous clothing made it even worse.

*   *   *

At the same time and whether a problem or a blessing, Reb was much smarter than her looks would suggest. Academically, she did very well in school. As her years in school progressed, her performance would place her further and further up the ladder as far as placement was concerned. Once she reached the top placement, she was surrounded by peers who were much more attractive, definitely more wealthy, and certainly much better dressed than she was. Many of her high-achieving peers came from families that were wealthy, were socially and often politically prominent, and were almost always the most popular and successful kids in school. From the sixth grade onward, Reb was a source of amusement and bullying by her peers, so much so that she would at times deliberately fail so that she could be with others who were more like her, at least in background. Rather than being proud of her intelligence, she hated it because it put her in a place where she was out of her element and couldn't compete. The 1960s and 1970s were not years that were particularly friendly to kids like her. She was ashamed of her poverty.

*   *   *

Reb's parents were good people who had grown up poor and knew no other way than working very hard, being frugal and careful. They had the best intentions. They loved their children and thought that they were providing their kids with a good upbringing, certainly better than what they had had themselves. Reb's parents encouraged and enforced a strong work ethic in their children. They expected that certain things would be done and done right, including school. Rules were to be followed. When her dad came home from a night's work, the children were expected to be quiet so that he could sleep for a few hours before going to his second job. In the early years, it was Reb's mother that was the caretaker and disciplinarian because her father was only there for a short time to sleep. He used whatever time off he had to work on repairing the old apartment house that he had bought and that they lived in. The problem was that Reb's mother was not a disciplinarian, and she couldn't control her oldest son's behavior. In fact, even she was scared of him.

The real problem and one of the reasons why her brother was never stopped was that this family never discussed anything. Never. Above all, routine, hard work, and achievement were the things that were expected and honored, just as her grandparents had done.

*　*　*

There was much that Reb never learned from her parents. Other than talking about very basic things, Reb's parents never encouraged talking. Every day was about schedule, accomplishment, and business. Reb never had a discussion with her mother about any of the things that girls experience as they grow up. She didn't know what a period was until she heard girls at school talk about it, lent another girl her sweater to wrap around her because of the obvious signs, and realized that this was something that other girls had, yet another thing that was important that she didn't have. She had to rely on her sister for information.

Even though Reb's brother had tried to teach her years earlier, she learned what sex really was and how babies were made from books, listening to friends, and talking to her sister. Whatever the problem, Reb listened, read, and learned to try to solve it herself. By living in an atmosphere that did not encourage questioning, Reb inferred that asking questions was a bad thing and that if she didn't know something or didn't know if something was right or wrong, she must be stupid.

If it couldn't be solved, it was to be endured with a genuine hope and prayer that somehow things would get better.

*   *   *

Thinking back, the lack of discussion and information from her parents was in some ways understandable. It had been the same for Reb's parents. They had had no guidance from their parents, but they had somehow forged ahead anyway. They were a product of the time in which they were raised, and now so were their children. Their own parents had been no different, and they had survived it and were working hard to do better.

Eventually, her parents did do better, just not during Reb's growing years. Reb's father would eventually achieve a certain degree of wealth, but it wouldn't happen until after all the children had grown, and the children would never see the benefit of that increased wealth, at least not during their childhood. They would all have to earn their own way just as their parents had done and just as their grandparents had done before them.

*   *   *

Given that her childhood home did not invite the truth when it really needed to be told, her earliest memories did not value discussion and sharing of ideas. It was all about achieving, accepting reality, and pushing for independence. Given this, a person of Reb's nature and intuition would see the reality of both of her parents, especially her mother. In Reb's young mind, it was her duty to protect those she saw as weaker than her, and her intuition told her that her mother would not be able to handle the truth. Her father would be too busy to be bothered. Part of Reb's reality was to learn to accept the beatings and the abuse and to never tell.

It was in this environment that Reb learned she was supposed to follow the rules, accomplish what was important, and yet still hold on to her need to survive. Even if it was a frightening situation, Reb didn't tell because it had long become second nature not to, and it wouldn't do any good if she did tell. She believed in the reality of her oldest brother's threats.

In a "do over," she would know better.

*   *   *

Because of the fear and the lack of communication, Reb, her youngest brother, and her sister were damaged in ways that were immeasurable and were never really resolved. They all survived in their own way and got out in their own way with hard work, higher education, brevity, and a determination to achieve. Her sister would become a successful scientist. Her youngest brother would become a very successful engineer and executive and travel all over the world.

Reb would become a speech therapist, a mistaken choice and not her first choice, but when on the path, she went for it as it was her built-in nature to always move forward.

All three would grow up to have very different personalities and viewpoints. All three would go through divorces, hardships, some tragedy, and hardest of all, challenges with their own children, but they would do so with the determination and resilience that had been instilled in them since a very young age. This was the positive part of their upbringing. They would survive. At the same time, they would be forever bonded by the abuse in the home that they had grown up in.

*   *   *

Her oldest brother had the same type of resilience. He would stay true to his nature. His abuse of Reb would go on until Reb was fourteen when he came home on leave from the army and Reb's mother finally put a stop to it, this time, not showing any fear or intimidation of her eldest son. Billy would go on to bully and abuse wives and children and cheat and lie his way into wealth, never paying for his actions, never showing any remorse. He would never acknowledge, feel any sense of guilt, or care about the bad things he had done, and he would never look back. Most of all, he never cared that the things he had done led him to later be rejected by his sisters and brother, but he would survive and, in fact, thrive, at least financially and materially. To Reb, to her youngest brother, and to her older sister, it wasn't fair, but it was what it was.

As an adult, Reb would work hard, pray, and learn to accept the unfairness. She tried very hard not to give her oldest brother any more of her energy or her life than what he had already taken, but this realization wouldn't come without a great deal of pain and anguish, and the memories of the nightmare he had created would keep coming back.

....

Over the years, Reb tried to simply wipe the slate clean. She couldn't. She tried very hard to come to a place of forgiveness and felt a great deal of guilt when she couldn't. She was a Christian, and it was what she had been taught was expected of her. It was what Jesus had done for her, and she was taught as a Christian to do the same. In her heart and soul, Reb wanted to forgive, and she really, really tried, but there was something, maybe a weakness in her, something . . . something that she couldn't control, something that would not allow her to forgive. She was too angry. She had been through too much and had kept so much to herself, so much inside. When she really understood what her oldest brother had done to her and what it had cost her, she just couldn't help it. She couldn't do it any longer. The anger and rage took over. She was as angry as she had ever been, and no matter how hard she tried, the anger would not go away.

This is the first time she ever really struck out at her parents, and it happened in the church parking lot during the one thing that Reb had been able to hang onto, choir practice.

*　　*　　*

Some people would call it ironic. Some people wouldn't understand. Some people would call it ridiculous. Reb's own sister could never understand.

*   *   *

Reb's relationship with her parents changed when she reached adulthood. It was a very gradual yet distinct change that Reb didn't recognize at the time, but she did as the years wore on. While her parents never spent money on such frivolous things as vacations or clothing when their children were growing up, they would be very supportive and helpful with their kids when the kids were adults. Part of it was because they had gained the wealth and security that they had worked so hard for. Part of it was because they were now in the position to do the right thing. Part of it was because just maybe they felt guilty. For whatever reason, Reb's parents were always there once she became an adult.

*   *   *

Reb spent her teen years working hard in school, earning good grades, working part-time jobs, and going in and out of the wrong crowds. She did things she wasn't proud of but got out of the wrong crowds when she knew she had to. She fell in love with a boy who would break her heart. She would marry very young, too young. She divorced, kept working, and kept going to school. She worked and paid her own way through four years of college. Reb would be the very first to go on to graduate school and earn a master's degree, something she would also pay for herself, the youngest child in her family, the youngest grandchild, and the first ever in her family to get this far—something she was very proud of at the time. Of course, the degree that she earned and the field that it led her into was not her first choice, a mistake of sorts but one she would have to make work for her. Even so, it was a tremendous accomplishment, just not an accomplishment that she would ever be able to relish in.

After Reb's very early marriage and divorce, she met a man at one of her part-time jobs. To put it simply, she fell hard and wanted to believe they were meant for each other. They weren't. In fact, for years afterward when she thought of him, he was nothing but a user, a liar, a ridiculously shallow person, an inconvenient reality, and yet another mistake. At the time, however, Reb was strongly attracted to him and him to her, and she built it into a romance that just wasn't there.

From the very start, the relationship was a rocky one. Other than physical attraction, they had nothing in common, and things would never grow beyond that point. What would grow was the baby that they made.

*   *   *

As the years passed, and her parents aged, Reb would become the caretaker and in many ways the matriarch of the family. It didn't happen all at once. It started with Reb's son.

*   *   *

When Reb found out she was pregnant, she was in graduate school and very much alone. She and the baby's father had broken up, and although they did try to get back together for a short time, the baby's father decided that he was too young for the responsibility and ended up abandoning Reb. At the time, Reb was furious with the abandonment, mortified at what she had done. She had been brought up in a home with an extended family that was Baptist, Christian. Even if her parents didn't bring their children up in the church, they did bring them up with very strict moral expectations. Being pregnant out of wedlock was something that just wasn't done and had never been done in her family, at least as far as she knew at the time. Given this, Reb wanted to be married when her baby was born. She didn't care if it ended up in divorce, but she wanted her child to be legitimate in the eyes of the law and God. This was deeply engrained in her, and when the baby's father didn't see it that way, she was truly devastated.

Reb's pregnancy was fairly normal, but it wasn't easy. It wasn't joyful as most impending mothers experience. It was full of uncertainty. For financial reasons, Reb chose to go with a midwife for the baby's birth. For her Lamaze class, Reb chose to ask a good friend to be her birthing partner. She didn't have anyone else. Her baby's father would have nothing to do with it. At the classes, Reb watched the other couples, husbands and wives, girlfriends and boyfriends, and she felt a deep sense of pain, the pain of being alone and scared and abandoned.

Reb had gone to many of her friend's baby showers, but her friends didn't give her one. In later years, she would drop these friends because she just couldn't forgive them for being so cruel. Her family didn't give her a baby shower. Only her fellow graduate students, who really didn't know her, did.

Even her grandmother, a woman Reb respected and adored, told her parents not to allow her to visit because she didn't want to answer any questions. Her youngest granddaughter was a source of shame.

Thank God, Reb's father didn't agree. This would be the beginning of a renewed trust between Reb and her parents.

*   *   *

While pregnant, Reb kept going to graduate school and working at her part-time jobs. She kept studying. Her father had let the rest of the family know that he was behind her. If Reb's grandmother and the rest of the family rejected her, he would reject them, and he meant it. So did Reb's mom. In the end, Reb's grandmother backed down, and Reb was grudgingly welcomed back into the fold. Even so, it was a wound that hurt Reb deeply, and she would never be quite as close to her grandmother again.

*   *   *

When Reb's son was born; her parents were her rock. They took Reb and the baby in when the baby's father abandoned ship. They gave Reb and her son shelter when she had no one else. As hard as Reb worked, she couldn't do it alone, and they were the reason that Reb was able to keep and raise her son. If it had not been for her parents, Reb would have been forced to give her son up, something she just couldn't do. Her son was her world and the most important thing in her life. Everything Reb did from that point onward was for her son.

It was the beginning of a special relationship between daughter and parents. Reb's parents adored their grandson, doted on him, and remained close to him throughout his growing years. From that point onward, Reb could always count of her parents to stand strong for her when she really needed them, and as time went on and her parents aged, they could always count on her to be there when needed. As an adult, she adored her parents and could never fathom having a time without them in her life. At the age of fifty-one, she was fortunate that she still had them both. But there were a few rocky times, especially when Reb learned the full breadth of what her oldest brother had done to her.

*   *   *

After Reb learned of the true nature of her injuries and health, she first went into a time of disbelief, but the disbelief didn't last for long. Next, she went into a period of anger and rage. She was angry at her oldest brother and for the first time in her life admitted to a feeling of actual hatred, something that certainly was not and would not be condoned by her church. But the anger didn't stop there. There was much more. She was angry that all the signs had been missed by the people who should have been looking out for her.

*   *   *

She was angry at the school that she worked at, the same school that she had attended as a child, now working with some of the teachers who had been working at the school when she was a child. In fact, in a matter of extreme irony, Reb had worked with a teacher who had been one of her favorites when she went to school, her third-grade teacher. This man had had all the children from Reb's family in his class. In even more extreme irony, when talking to this teacher many years later, the only one he could remember was her oldest brother, asking how her brother was doing and telling her about incidents he had had with her brother and how her brother was so smart. At the time, Reb had had to maintain a professional mask and showed no reaction on the outside. On the inside, she was seething. After all, it was during her third-grade year that the worst of the sexual abuse happened.

After finding out the true breadth of what her oldest brother had done to her, Reb had a great deal of difficulty even being around her former third-grade teacher. Apparently, she had just been a quiet little wallflower who worked hard and got good grades, nothing special and nothing worth remembering. Reb was very angry that this teacher and everyone else in the school never recognized the signs.

As an adult in her teaching job, Reb would learn that this particular teacher actually had an enormous ego himself, tended to only be interested in the welfare of his male students and often was impatient with his female students. She was glad when this teacher finally retired and she no longer had to appear to like him.

* * *

Most of all, however, Reb was angry with her parents. She loved them dearly and didn't want to blame them, yet they hadn't protected her. They hadn't protected her youngest brother. They hadn't protected her sister. They had had a violent, deranged son in their home that they had tried to cope with but ultimately failed their other children by not either getting him some help or getting him out of the home. Because of this, her legs were fractured. Her pelvis was fractured. She had broken ribs, and she had been sexually molested. Her youngest brother had fared only a little better than she, and her sister would grow up and never forgive.

*   *   *

When Reb began going through the rage and hurt of what had been done to her, she began to avoid her parents. For weeks, she could not and would not go near them. After not hearing from her for so long, Reb's dad went to the church where he knew she would be at choir practice. He wanted to tell her something important. She didn't give him the chance. This was the first time she struck out at her parents, and she blasted him.

"I told you a long time ago what Billy did to me, but you didn't believe it, or you didn't want to believe it. You know why I'm walking with a cane? Do you know why I'm so tired and in so much pain? Because Billy beat the shit out of me so badly when I was a kid that he broke my legs. Do you know why I couldn't have Alex naturally? Because your son broke my pelvis. He broke my ribs. He did exactly what I told you he did, and now I've paid for it with my body. And yes, he really did the sexual stuff that I told you about, more than once. I didn't lie. I wouldn't lie, not about something like this. I want that bastard to know what he did, and I want you to tell him. I never want anything to do with him again. He is out of my life, and I won't have any part in anything involving him. I want this family to own up to all of it. It happened, and I never lied!"

Reb then cancelled the family Christmas celebration or at least her part in it. Once her sister learned what had happened, she too rejected Billy and stood by her sister.

Reb's father did, in fact, tell Billy about Reb's condition. Billy responded by having a letter sent to her from his lawyer. In the letter, his lawyer threatened Reb with a lawsuit for defamation of character, telling her to cease and desist all talk of allegations of incest and abuse on the part of her client. Reb responded by writing her own letter, one that stated she had the medical proof and basically to bring it on; she was ready. Reb was through being threatened. She never heard from the lawyer again.

*   *   *

At that point in time, the family would never be together as a whole again. There would come a time when Reb would become convinced that her parents didn't really believe her, or at least that her father didn't, that they were just trying to keep the peace and that ultimately she was being held responsible for the split in the family. Once convinced of her parents' disbelief, Reb became yet again very angry and steadfast in her feeling that she had been hurt enough, had protected enough, and wasn't going to be a victim any longer. She would never back down and would never have anything to do with her oldest brother again. When she thought that her parents did not believe her, she stuck to her guns and let them know that if they didn't believe her, she simply did not want to be a part of the family any longer. She was ready to go her own way.

*   *   *

Her mother would eventually accept that Reb was telling the truth and would often tell Reb how sorry she was and wished that she would have done things differently. Reb's mother would eventually be even more honest, telling her that she really had been scared of Billy and would have and should have had Billy removed from the home had she and Reb's father known the true reality of what he had done. This helped Reb in her road to acceptance and forgiveness.

Reb's father, however, would never allow himself to fully accept the truth. He never said so because he loved and needed his daughter and was afraid that she would abandon them, but Reb knew. In time, she also understood.

*   *   *

Over the years, Reb had seen the pain and heard it in her father's voice whenever he talked about his family. Even at the age of eighty-one, there was still a glint of a tear when he talked about being rejected, neglected, and abused by his father and stepmother, never knowing his mother and being shut out of his family. The type of abuse that he had lived through was different than Reb's, but abuse was abuse, and the memories last forever. Like Reb, her father never passed on the abuse to his own. He just never faced the fact that one of his own would pass it on anyway.

In time, knowing her father and his own history of abuse, Reb would understand that her father simply could never and would never come to a place of believing that the son who most looked like him could ever do such a terrible thing. There was a part of her father that could not abandon one of his children, no matter what. He could not abandon one of his own as he had been abandoned, even for the right reason. Reb would and did come to a place of forgiveness and acceptance where her father was concerned. Abuse had done its job on him as well.

*   *   *

Reb would try very hard yet never be able to forgive her oldest brother, but she would come to a point of acceptance, or so she thought. Her brother never acknowledged what he had done, and Reb would learn to accept that he never would. She learned to accept that in reality, he was a very evil person, maybe something handed down from her father's family but evil nonetheless. It happened in this world, and sometimes people like her brother never paid for the things they did, at least not in this life.

In later years, Reb's mother was convinced that her eldest son had either blocked out the memories of what he had done to his siblings or had reinvented the facts to make a new truth that absolved him. Reb's sharp instinct told her that while that might be a possibility, it was more likely a matter of time passing, her oldest brother being at a point of wealth and safety in his life and for the most part, just not giving a damn. Somehow, life had given him what he wanted and to hell with the wreckage he left behind.

....

Yet again, Reb's acceptance or the measure of acceptance she achieved allowed her to move on. She would never again give her oldest brother the level of rage and anger that she had felt when she realized he had fractured her legs and taken away her ability to have children. He just wasn't worth it, and he had taken enough. At this point, Reb yet again tried to move on and live her life. Not that life would be any easier. It wasn't. Things would get worse, and life would continue to be difficult. Reb would lose her first career.

*   *   *

Reb's first career wasn't her choice. It was chosen by a guidance counselor's incompetence. Reb had always been interested in teaching, especially in working with the deaf. In high school, she had even taken adult night school to learn sign language. She loved the courses, did well, and became proficient. When it was time to begin looking at college, she went to her guidance counselor, told him what she wanted to do, and asked him what courses or college she would need to attend. He told her that she needed to first earn a bachelor's degree in communication disorders or speech and language therapy. Next, she would need to go to graduate school and earn a degree in the education of the deaf. He was wrong, but Reb didn't know it at the time.

At the age of seventeen, like her grandmother before her, Reb began attending the University of Maine at Farmington but in her case with a major in speech communication disorders and a minor in elementary education. She lived in a dorm, and her first roommate was a girl who was deaf. Ironically, she and her first roommate didn't hit it off. Her roommate was a party girl, and Reb was one of the few students who didn't party. She was paying her own way through college and had to work hard. She worked as much as she could in work-study jobs and learned more from the jobs than her courses. By the second semester of her freshman year, Reb would have a new roommate, a very special friend named Leigh who would become a lifelong friend.

Reb struggled with certain subjects and excelled at others, especially the science and speech therapy-related courses. She had some great times during her freshman and sophomore years in college and made some very good friends. She joined the college chorus and was a part of the theater. These were very good times for Reb. It was the first time and one of the only times in her life that she felt strong and free. Yet even with this, Reb was homesick, and by the middle of her sophomore year, she was lovesick.

*   *   *

Reb had known her first husband when she was a kid. He was part of one of the groups of kids that she later removed herself from because she didn't like the things that they did. He too had come from a very dysfunctional family. They had lost contact and met again when Reb was eighteen, during the summer following her freshman year in college, the summer of 1979. At the time, Reb was working as a work-study student in a local hospital, a job she absolutely loved. Derrick was in the army and home on leave. By the time Reb saw Derrick again, she was nearly nineteen and had grown into a fairly attractive young woman, not in body, which was still very thin, but in her face, which would always be her best asset. The biggest change had been in her personality. She was no longer the quiet, mousy, shy twelve-year-old Derrick had known years before. This Reb was outgoing and sure of herself, at least in what she showed to the world. She was very different from the girl he had known before. Derrick was no longer the small, wild kid he had been but a tall, handsome grown man of twenty who was also changed. The two of them were attracted to each other immediately.

Reb and Derrick dated during the month that he was home on leave. After that, they kept in contact by writing letters. Reb went back to college where she worked hard and lived another year in the dorm. Back overseas, Derrick sent her presents, lots of presents. Each day in the dorm, Reb went to her mailbox, hoping for a letter, and she was almost never disappointed. When Derrick finished his tour of duty and got out of the army, Reb was there to welcome him home. Once home, Reb went home every weekend to see Derrick as he settled into civilian life. By April of 1980, they were engaged to be married. Reb transferred to the university closest to her home, and she and Derrick were married in July.

They were both so young and immature that the marriage never had a chance.

For a variety of reasons, the marriage lasted only about a year and a half. Afterward, Reb continued to go to college and worked two to three part-time jobs. She lived in many places, with her parents, with a very special aunt, and eventually alone in her own apartment. She continued to major in speech communication disorders, but she would learn that her major was not the road to her ultimate goal as she found out that she needed a different degree. The problem was that she was paying her own way, responsible for taking care of herself, and could not afford to back up; she was too close to earning her bachelor's degree. So Reb moved forward, continued on, graduated with a bachelor's degree in communication disorders and went on to graduate school in speech pathology. It was during the first year of graduate school that she met her son's father, engaged in a relationship that was doomed from the beginning and had a baby during the last semester of her second year in graduate school. She graduated with a master's degree in speech/language pathology in August of 1984. She was twenty-three, a single mother and entering into the professional arena as a speech pathologist. It wasn't what she really wanted to do, but she had a son to support, and he was going to have the best that she could provide. He was her life.

*   *   *

Reb chose to work in the schools. As a single mother, she didn't have the time or money to do what it took to be licensed for either private practice or work in a hospital, nor was she interested. She had always enjoyed working with special needs children and working in the schools ensured it. Working in schools also required only that she maintain state certification which would take only six credit hours every five years, and the course work was paid for by the school department.

In August of 1984, Reb was hired by a school district in southern Maine. It would require that she move a long way from home without the support of her parents, but she had to do it in order to get her foot in the door. Reb's salary as a first-year teacher was below the poverty line. It was an extremely tough year for her in many ways, but in others, it was a growing and strengthening time. She became very independent, resilient, and most important of all, even more determined to do the best that she could for her son. It was just her and Alex that year, and he was the focal point in her life. In that year, as frightened as she was, Reb learned to stand on her own two feet. In that year, Reb also learned how important her family was. There were many desperate times, times when her father and mother came to the rescue and one very special time when her sister and her sister's new husband did the same.

In 1985, Reb's income as a first-year teacher was so low that it simply could not provide all the basic necessities. Reb was a single mother who received no child support from the baby's father and no welfare. In that area of the state and in the town she worked in, housing for single mothers was extremely limited. In reality, single mothers like her were rare and almost unheard of in this single-family suburb of Portland. Low income housing did not exist in this area, and Reb was not going to live in Portland by herself with a baby. Reb ended up renting a beautiful little cottage on Sebago Lake. It was a winterized summer rental with the landlords living in a large house next door. The cottage was at the end of a camp road. The inside was furnished, open, and spacious enough for a mother and her infant son. Reb needed only to bring the nursery, her clothes, and items for the kitchen. It was quiet and safe. The lake was breathtaking. It was a great place to escape to at the end of a long day of work. The problem was it was also expensive.

Reb had to pay rent, childcare, electricity, phone, fuel, a car payment, food and clothing for her child. She had little professional clothing for herself and had to make due with what little she had. One of her biweekly paychecks did little more than pay her rent for the month. Childcare took up half of the next biweekly check, and Reb did her best to make whatever was left over take care of the rest. On the few weekends that she was able to make it home, Reb's parents took care of her son so that she could work at the local library to make a little extra income. Reb's mother did her laundry and gave her some money to help. Alex's other grandparents paid for a diaper plan and gave Reb a generous monetary Christmas gift.

*   *   *

Maine winters can be brutal, and even when not brutal, they are always cold. In February of 1985, Reb found herself in probably the most desperate circumstances she would ever be in. Even with all the help her parents and Alex's other grandparents had given, Reb found herself out of money and nearly out of heating oil with a baby to protect. She found herself with limited food for her son and almost no food for herself. It was a tough choice. Reb made the decision to use whatever money she had to put oil in the tank. She could only hope that her family would be there for her again, yet again, although she didn't tell them.

For whatever inexplicable reason, the very next day, her sister, her wonderful sister, and her wonderful brother-in-law came to her door from a two-hour drive with bags and bags of groceries, two of them filled with baby food and the rest filled with food and things that Reb needed. It was an act of kindness that Reb would never forget.

There were other acts of incredible kindness from her family and from others during that year. At the time, her father was still working for the FAA and was responsible for checking and reviewing the lighting systems for most of the airports in Maine. During this year, her father would use every excuse to travel south and drop in on his daughter and grandson, staying the night and making sure that everything was okay. In December of 1984, just three weeks before Christmas, her father dropped in. In his hands was a Charlie Brown tree with its bottom nailed to a wooden platform, just tall enough to be placed on the kitchen table out of the reach of a very curious and active eleven-month-old. In years to come, Reb would have a lot of Christmas trees, most full, tall, and beautiful, but there would never be a tree as beautiful as that one.

When home for Christmas, Reb's mother had asked her to try on a coat that she had bought for Reb's grandmother. The coat fit and looked good. "It's yours, from your grandmother." Reb had been wearing a very old threadbare coat that barely kept out the cold.

Alex's paternal grandparents had given her 100 dollars for Christmas. With this, Reb was able to buy presents for her son's first Christmas and have his portrait taken.

Reb's coworkers, even though they did not know her well, gave her beautiful clothing for her son and helped to get her out of the house once in a while complete with babysitting and borrowed clothing for Reb.

Her parents paid for the repairs on her car.

Yes, it was a tough year but a healing year and the year in which Reb began to believe in herself. It was the year that connected her to her son in a way that could never be broken. Much of the time was spent alone, just the two of them, and they became each other's world. Both of their worlds would continue to expand, and there would be many rocky times in the future. Alex had a spark and a unique and independent nature that was all his own. It was in this very first year, when neither of them really had anyone but each other, that Reb became stronger and realized what a true miracle she had been given.

*　　*　　*

In time, Reb was able to do her income tax and would earn enough in a tax refund to make the rest of that particular year something she could survive.

*   *   *

During that year, Reb also began to really hone her skills as a speech therapist. It was during this first year of teaching that she began to show a true instinct and talent as a teacher. It would take a lot longer for her to trust these skills, but they were there nonetheless.

*   *   *

At the end of her first year of teaching and away from home, Reb landed what she thought was her dream job. She was hired by the school system in the city where she had grown up. In fact, she was hired at the very elementary school that she had gone to as a child. She was thrilled and moved back in with her parents until she was able to have her own place again.

*   *   *

Over the years, Reb would hone and improve her skills as a speech therapist and teacher. She would remarry at the age of twenty-six and go on to provide the best that she could for her son and her husband. She would remain working for the school department and over time gain prestige and a certain amount of power. She would become particularly adept at her more administrative duties such as being a special education coordinator. She became the best at running meetings, taking the minutes of meetings, generating reports, and handling difficult situations. She was the first to use a word processor for paperwork and the first to help develop and pilot a special education database, before it became commonplace. She became so good at her job that in time she was the dumping ground for everyone's problems and issues, both professional and personal. Should a crisis happen and the principal not be there, she was designated as the one to be in command.

*   *   *

Over the years, Reb had many challenging students that she was very proud of. While working at the high school as her secondary placement, Reb worked with a girl who had been mute from the age of six and who, under Reb's guidance, would become verbal and eventually become a successful adult. She had worked with a very special boy with such severe cerebral palsy that he had no intelligible speech but who would become understandable under her guidance. She worked with an autistic boy who spoke in unintelligible jargon but who would later be completely understandable and make straight A's in school. Finally, she would work with an entire family of girls with unintelligible speech who would be clearly understood by the time they left Reb's school, and each of them would go on to be successful. These were the most memorable ones, but Reb would work with hundreds of students over the years and be successful in helping most of them. The tough ones were the ones she relished the most, the ones she would always be challenged to try to find a way to give them the time that they needed, even though she usually had far more students than she could handle.

This kind of success did not come without a price. Reb's hours were long, often twelve hours or more a day. The job was intense, stressful, and on her mind twenty-four hours a day, even in her dreams. For ten months out of the year, she could never let it go. She somehow fit the rest of her life around it, but the job always took precedence, not that she wanted it that way. It was just the reality of teaching. She did the best that she could to meet the needs of her family, but it was never enough. Her son was a challenge. Her husband was a challenge. Her parents were a challenge, and eventually, her youngest brother would be a challenge as well.

The one saving grace was that her job eventually paid well and combined with her husband's wages, Reb and her husband were able to achieve some of their dreams, a house, decent vehicles, and occasional vacation. Reb could lavish her son with material things, clothes, toys, special activities. She could be generous with everyone on Christmas and other special occasions. For years, she and her husband held the major holidays for the whole family in their home, and they were often large and expensive events. In many ways, these were good years. Things were always moving forward, and they felt safe.

*   *   *

That safety would begin to erode when Reb's health took a turn for the worse. Reb's job had always been difficult and exhausting. She had always been somewhat frail and had had periods of weakness and illness that made working difficult. Working in the public schools, she was constantly exposed to flu and colds, and as a speech therapist, she worked in close contact with young children who were often coughing or sneezing in her face. Once ill, Reb would remain sick much longer than the average person and would usually have to go to the doctor to get an antibiotic that would put her back on her feet. She was almost never able to suffer through an illness without medical attention. Because of this, Reb sometimes missed work that she didn't want to miss and was pressured by the school district not to miss the time. Her job was unusual, unique, and there was no substitute to take her place when she wasn't there. For years, Reb felt the stress of never being allowed to suffer from a common illness like other people could and always having to justify any time that she wasn't at work. In time, Reb realized that while she might be respected for the job that she did, the people that she worked with or for, no matter how long she had worked with them, they really didn't care about her as a person. Even so, Reb was dedicated, and she always went back as quickly as she could.

When Reb began having difficulty with her walking because of the injuries from childhood, she also had less and less endurance. She walked with a cane and had little energy. She couldn't work with certain students without having someone else there because she couldn't protect herself in case of violence or catch a child if they bolted. The stress and the negative parts of her job began to take more and more of a toll on her. She missed more and more work to the point where she ran out of sick time. There came a time where she could no longer put her students first and could not cope. Worst of all, when she could no longer cope, she lost the ability to care. By the time Reb was forty-eight and after twenty-four years of teaching, she couldn't do it any longer. She had to quit.

*   *   *

The truth was that Reb was forced into retiring early because of the injuries that she had sustained in childhood. The truth also was that Reb had always hated the job, and if this hadn't come along to wear her down, something else would have.

*   *   *

Reb had never really wanted to be a speech therapist, and she certainly had never gone into the field to deal with the problems that she would have to deal with, all the things that were really outside of actually teaching the children. Like many teachers, and Reb did consider herself a teacher, only a different kind, she would come to realize that in society, she and other teachers like her were people who had the best intentions but who would often be treated like indentured servants by people on the outside and by the administrators and school board members. Lip service as to how wonderful they all were was always paid to school employees on the first and last day of each school year by the very people who expected the impossible for all the days in between while never giving the teachers the backing and support that they both needed and deserved. She would be told time and time again how lucky she was to have her summers off. She would be treated with disdain and disrespect by parents who used the school platform not to advocate for their children but to focus on their own mistrust and their own issues. She would work overtime, a lot of overtime, writing reports that would be put under a microscope by these same distrusting parents. She would work night after night, week after week, and month after month of writing IEPs, PET minutes, evaluation reports, classroom observation reports, progress reports, and plans without pay. She worked under the expectations of layers of administrators, some competent, some not, some reasonable, some arrogant, some bullying; and as in most places, she worked with some professional equals who were bullies themselves, one in particular.

*   *   *

In truth, the job really was the job from hell. After a certain special education teacher was hired and an equally bullying special education director came on board, Reb would secretly refer to her primary school placement and school department as her little shop of horrors. She learned never to be surprised by anything that happened, and she never changed her opinion.

Yet Reb was devoted to the children and to the financial security it gave her family. As long as she was healthy, she was always able to separate the goals and pride she had in her students from the crap that the rest of her job entailed, and she could almost always put on a calm face in the face of chaos, never really showing how she felt.

As long as she was healthy, she and her husband could provide well for Alex and could live comfortably. After her son graduated from high school in 2002, Reb and her husband enjoyed a few years of financial security, took a dream vacation, and had work done on their home that would turn the house into something close to what they had both hoped for. Sadly, Reb's health was compromised by her fractured legs, pelvis, and dwindling strength and energy. It was inevitable that she would have to retire early.

As her health declined, Reb knew that she would not last in her career. At the same time, she was angry that her brother had taken so much from her and was determined to, in her sister's words, "make lemonade out of lemons." Reb did not want what her brother had done to keep her from working and achieving. She did not want to go on disability. She just didn't want to give him the satisfaction even if he didn't care one way or the other.

*   *   *

While still working as a teacher, Reb began to research fields that would use talents she had and that she really enjoyed. Reb was fairly competent with computers. She had excellent keyboarding skills and a facility for language and writing. Most of all, she wanted to do something that would limit walking and could be done at home. She found all this in the field of medical transcription.

*   *   *

In June 2008, at the age of forty-eight, Reb officially retired from teaching. Some would only call it a resignation, but after thirty years, six years of training, and twenty-four years of devoted service, it was a retirement. Reb immediately began an online training program in medical transcription. She enjoyed her early months of retirement enormously. For the first time in many years, Reb felt calm and rested.

For the next eleven months, Reb worked hard and obtained her certificate of completion in May of 2009. It wasn't easy. Being so much older and learning a brand-new field of study was harder than Reb expected. Her mind wasn't as agile or quick as it had been when she was in her teens and twenties. She had also forgotten how difficult it could be to enter a profession as a person without experience, even if her work and life experience were rich.

Reb had also forgotten how it felt to be financially constrained. She and her husband struggled with the money issues, really struggled, but Reb loved the work and eventually landed her first job. The job wasn't financially rewarding, but just as in her teaching days, it did get her foot in the door and gave her the experience she really needed. She loved the work and was a natural at it.

*   *   *

During this time, Reb had another issue to deal with. Her family became more and more needy and required more and more of her time and care. Her mother's health declined. Her father's health declined, and Reb spent much of her free time caring for her parents. As of August of 2009, Reb also had her brother to deal with.

* * *

Reb's youngest brother, Sammy, was actually two years older than she was. He was the third in the birth order. Reb was the fourth and the youngest. Reb's oldest brother was the second in the birth order and five years older than Reb. Her sister was the first in the birth order and seven years older than Reb. In childhood, Reb was never close to her sister other than in a mixture of adoration and jealousy. Reb's oldest brother, Billy, was large, strong, and a living nightmare to live with. Sammy had always been her saving grace.

For the first ten years of her life, Reb roomed with her youngest brother, an unusual situation by today's standards but necessary at the time because there weren't enough bedrooms for everyone to have their own. Both of her older siblings had their own room. Reb's parents had their room. She and Sammy shared a room. The room was large and had a set of bunk beds. Reb fondly remembered her brother demanding that she close her eyes and put her head under the covers so that he could change into his pajamas, even though he was on the top bunk and she couldn't see anything anyway. As children, they would sneak around the house before Christmas, trying to find presents. Each Christmas Eve, they would stay awake all night listening for Santa's reindeer and swear that they heard him land on the roof. Reb's youngest brother, Sammy, was the only one that she felt she could really trust. She adored him, and they were the best of friends.

Her youngest brother was a go-getter, impulsive, a bit nuts at times, and very active. He was always very friendly, a true people person. He was two years ahead of Reb in school but would take Reb along in many of his adventures. As teenagers, Sammy included Reb in some of his world. Some of the best times Reb ever had had happened when she was a sophomore in high school and her brother was a senior.

Sammy was the exact opposite of her oldest brother. He was shorter and smaller like Reb. In fact, he and Reb looked quite a bit alike. He was also kind and would never intentionally hurt another person. He was respectful of his parents and a friend to both of his sisters. If he could, he would help anyone in anyway.

The worst thing that Reb and Sammy shared in common was that they both had been severely beaten many times by their oldest brother. Sammy would also end up with permanent emotional scars and physical injuries from what his brother had done to him.

Sammy would grow up and go on to be very successful. He left home right after graduation and made his own way. He put himself through college. In the years to come, he would become a high-level executive in the earlier days of the computer industry and would travel all over the world. He would become a licensed pilot. He would also marry, go through a divorce, remarry, and divorce again.

Sammy would make a tremendous amount of money. He would finance his parents' fiftieth anniversary, a grand and expensive affair that Reb loved planning, an evening that her parents and the rest of the family would never forget and the last time that the entire family, including Billy, would ever be together.

*   *   *

Sammy would live his life with a passion. Where Reb was on the quiet and reserved side, Sammy was gregarious, outgoing, and unpredictable. He would bring his sons up with love and with the best of material things and, like Reb, work hard at being a good parent. He was a source of pride for the family and would live the high life, until something struck him down.

In 2002, Sammy was diagnosed with lupus, a disease that typically occurs in women but when diagnosed in men is particularly vicious and not well understood by the medical community. He had had real problems with pain, fatigue, and mental ability for months before the actual diagnosis, but he didn't tell his family. He had the classic symptoms of the disease, but because he was a male, the doctors didn't test for it. Finally, one doctor was willing to look outside the box, had the biopsies done, and correctly diagnosed the disease. From that point on, life would change drastically. It would be a very long time until Sammy was able to accept and live with his illness. There would be many hospitalizations, many surgeries, and many emergencies.

*   *   *

Lupus is a disease that isn't understood by many, not even the medical community though most would like to think that they do. Unlike cancer, diabetes, and HIV, it has never received the research and money needed to understand the disease, try to find a cure, much less management of the disease; and for her brother and the rest of the family, it was very scary territory. They were often flying by the seat of their pants and quickly learned that they could not count on the medical community.

Lupus is an autoimmune disease that is the direct opposite of AIDS but not sexually transmitted or in fact transmitted in any way. With AIDS, the autoimmune process is depressed and not functioning, allowing even the most common cold to turn into a deadly disease. With lupus, the autoimmune system is in overdrive and sees the body as a virus that it must attack. It attacks the bodies' major organs, the skin, the heart, the lungs, the kidneys, the vascular system, the skeletal system, the joints, the eyes, the ears, the brain. You name the organ, and lupus may attack.

The most fortunate people with lupus have only the skin form of the disease, a butterfly rash, and a sensitivity to sunlight. Many others have the form of the disease that affects the skin, joints, and vascular system, which is when it really gets painful. The most unfortunate are those that have the worst form of the disease, the type that attacks the major organs as well as the skin and joints. Reb's brother had that form, and it was truly catastrophic.

*   *   *

During the early years of Sammy's disease, Reb, her husband, and her parents would travel to New Hampshire as often as they could. In the early years, Reb would go to her brother's home and do whatever she could. Sometimes, she would bring one or both of her parents. At other times, her sister and brother-in-law would travel down. Each visit was for a different reason, sometimes because he was in the hospital, sometimes to take him to a hospital, and sometimes just to be there.

Her brother had been wise. Well, before he was diagnosed and had any idea of how sick he was, Sammy had purchased and paid a high premium for a disability plan through his company. He also qualified for social security disability. For a few years, this helped him hold on to his home and possessions, but his income, even with the higher disability income, was far less than what he had made during his career, and his expenses were consistent with someone who made six figures.

Sammy was also living with a debilitating disease that robbed him of clear thinking, and he made a lot of bad decisions. The doctors did a good job of treating his pain, but they also helped him to sleep through his days by prescribing drugs that sedated him. His disease was progressive and would present with different challenges, seizures, broken bones, torn joints, cognitive and memory issues. Stress was the worst, and stress of any kind would make any symptoms he experienced one hundred times worse.

For several years, Reb and different members of her family would travel to New Hampshire as often as they could and help in any way that they could. Sammy was steadfast and determined to remain in the home that he so loved in the place that he so loved, and with his disability plan, he was able to maintain his home as his world, at least for a while.

His boys were not a lot of help to him. The younger one was strong with a great personality and a source of pride for the whole family, a United States Marine who would ultimately be deployed in Iraq or Afghanistan not once, twice, three or four times, but five times. Yet despite all that this young Marine did and experienced, he was simply too immature and wild to give his father the kind of care that he needed.

The older son was selfish and self-centered, completely materialistic and often cruel, much like Reb's oldest brother who also never did anything to help his brother.

*   *   *

After several years, Reb's parents aged in such a way that they could no longer make the trip. Her mother could not navigate the stairs at Sammy's house. Her father could no longer drive the distance. Most of all, Reb was too sick to drive anything more than a few miles at a time and could not make the three-hundred-mile trip. There were times when she tried but had to turn back because she was so ill and weak. For a while, only Reb's sister and husband were able to make the trip, and it was taxing on them as well.

For years, offers had been made to Sammy to bring him home. Understandably, he had lost so much and wanted to remain in the place that he loved, so he had declined. Now, however, his family was nearly as challenged as he was.

*   *   *

When Reb retired early from teaching, she did it for a number of reasons, first and foremost that her health simply wouldn't allow her to do the job the way that it needed to be done. When she retired, she thought she had chosen a new career that would allow her to use her talents, earn a decent income, and give her time for her family, something that teaching never allowed. At the time, she was most concerned about her aging parents who needed a lot of support and time from her, and while she was always worried about her younger brother, there was little that she could do any longer for him other than talk with him on the phone. That would change by the summer of 2009.

*   *   *

In May of 2009, Reb completed her training in medical transcription and received the proper certificate. In August of 2009, she was hired by a company that would give a new MT a chance. In June of 2009, her brother called her asking if she would help him move home, back to Maine. He had been through hell and back. Things were desperate, and he was ready to come home.

During the previous two or three years, Sammy had gone through even more trauma, terrible things. His disease kept landing him in the hospital. One of his hospitalizations resulted in him acquiring MRSA or methicillin-resistant Staphylococcus aureus, a highly contagious infection that was difficult and often painful to treat. He and his girlfriend of many years had broken up. He became the victim of identity theft when a so-called friend found his social security number and did many thousands of dollars of damage before he was caught and stopped. Given all that her brother had gone through, Sammy was finally forced into bankruptcy and lost his beloved home.

*   *   *

On August 1, 2009, Reb, her husband, and a crew of their friends traveled to New Hampshire, loaded a large moving truck, and moved her brother home. Reb had rented a house for her brother about a mile from her own home, an old derelict house that was over-priced but had the necessary components her brother needed, including a fenced-in backyard for his beloved dog, Duke.

Reb had not seen her brother in many months, and when she first saw her brother, she was shocked. He was very thin and very sick, so sick that she feared for his life. Once home and set up in his rental home, Sammy would go through three more hospitalizations. On two occasions, Reb would check on her brother and find him either comatose or nearly so and call an ambulance. Reb would arrange for all his medical providers, schedule the appointments, and take him to each one. It was a learning process, and she made mistakes.

During the week, Reb and her husband cooked and brought down daily meals for Sammy. During the weekends when Reb and her husband were off, they brought Sammy to their home and cared for him there.

When Sammy was hospitalized, Reb would spend as much time as she could at the hospital and would advocate for her brother when she felt that people were not doing the right thing, which was often. Reb's innate distrust of the medical community would only be reinforced, and she would be challenged to be patient.

Reb would learn that the medical community was suspicious and unforgiving of mistakes and that when a doctor made a judgment, even a wrong one, it stuck and would create a lot of problems. During the first year of Sammy being home, Reb would learn to distrust just about all the doctors she encountered. She learned that once an opinion was formed, doctors did not listen to patients or their family members and that they would steadfastly and stubbornly refuse to change their opinions regardless of the facts or what their decisions would do to the patient. Much of what she heard in her new career as a medical transcriptionist would not change this opinion. Once stated in a report, the information would be passed along whether wrong or right.

During the first year that her brother was home, he would be accused of being a drug addict. He wasn't and Reb knew it. Her brother had been on narcotics for years for the extreme pain that his disease caused and if this made him dependent, so be it. It was understandable. Yet her brother was not only considered to be dependent but drug seeking and he would be labeled and treated no differently than the drug seekers who took the narcotics simply to get high. Her brother was unstable but he wasn't an addict, not in the traditional sense, and he certainly wasn't drug seeking. However, Sammy's medical care in the state of Maine was occurring during a time of extreme paranoia where prescribing narcotics was concerned. Anyone receiving narcotics for pain management was painted with the same brush and her brother apparently was an easy target. It was even postulated by hospital doctors that he was going out seeking drugs that he wasn't prescribed. Sammy wasn't and Reb knew it but convincing doctors of this was futile. Time and time again, Reb tried to explain to the doctors that her brother was too sick and did not go out into the community as he was most often confined to his home.

Reb had long since taken on the responsibility of measuring out his medications on a daily basis and knew exactly what he was taking and how much. Yes, mistakes were made but they were honest mistakes and never even in the ballpark of what both Sammy and Reb would be suspected of or accused of. They were simply mistakes with no ulterior motive. However, once labeled it was impossible to convince anyone otherwise. Things would only get worse.

*   *   *

During one of Sammy's hospitalizations, he complained of extreme pain in his leg. He was told by the doctor on duty that "lupus doesn't cause that kind of pain" and was again accused of drug seeking.

Reb would learn the helplessness of dealing with a system and a medical community that were impossible to deal with. She watched her brother's anger escalate as he continued to be subjected to false allegations, incorrect assumptions and a lack of competency by the very people who were supposed to be treating him.

On this particular hospitalization, after all the pain that her brother endured and all the drama, one doctor finally ordered a simple test. It turned out that Sammy had a very large clot in his leg that accounted for the pain and in reality could have killed him.

Of course, no apology or retraction was ever given by any of the doctors. Reb was appalled at the arrogance of the doctors and lost respect for the profession, yet again. From this point on, both Sammy and Reb would avoid the hospital as much as possible, a frightening point of view for a man with such a severe illness and his caretaking perpetually weakened sister.

*   *   *

During that first year of Sammy being home, Reb would also help him through his bankruptcy proceedings and be there whenever she could to help him through the stress of adjusting to the move. They were tough times, but things would get better.

In time, some good things would happen. There would be changes in outpatient doctors and a reduction in certain medications, particularly the medications that were making him sleep through his disease and dull his ability to think for himself. As his mental clarity began to return, Sammy was able to make some decisions better and become seizure-free which would allow him to drive again. Once through his bankruptcy, he was able to begin handling a lot of the day-to-day stresses without panic attacks. He would take himself off narcotics and learn to deal with his pain in other ways. Yes, he did smoke marijuana from time to time, which Reb supported, even if she didn't do it herself.

In time, Reb and her husband no longer had to bring down daily meals as Sammy became more and more able to do for himself. Sammy gained weight, became much stronger, and eventually handled all of his own medical appointments. In time, Sammy was able to help out in emergencies where his parents were concerned, and he was there for Reb when she had her down times. By August of 2011, he was ready to get rid of his rental house and the high rent, dispose of the possessions that he didn't need or use, and move on. Sadly, Duke, Sammy's precious yellow lab, had died the previous November.

In September of 2011, Sammy moved in with some friends on a beautiful horse farm, learned how to take care of the horses, helped his friends with their business, and looked healthier and happier than he had in many, many years. He still had difficult days with his disease, but things were much, much better for him.

*　　*　　*

The truth was that Sammy had come home to die, yet somehow, he had found the strength to come back and begin to live again. Reb was proud of her brother. He was the most courageous person she had ever known.

*   *   *

During the years of 2010 and 2011, Reb's mother's health also declined, severely declined. In 2011, her mother would be hospitalized three times and be in two nursing homes, all in the course of about five months. During that time, Reb would alternate between caring for and advocating for her mother, checking on her father, taking care of her brother, checking in with her son who lived far away, depending on her husband who worked a lot of overtime, and working a full-time evening shift herself with overtime. Like her brother, Reb's mother would eventually improve with the right combination of medications, care, and her mother's own determination. Reb was able to do it all precisely because her job was a job that she could truly leave when her time was done, but she and her husband were constantly overstressed and tired. Reb could only deal with it all a day at a time, and she was hanging on by a thread.

*   *   *

On August 5, 2011, Reb was in the garden weeding with the use of an old garden weasel that she had used for years. As usual, Reb had allowed the weeds and the grass in the garden to get ahead of her, and she was trying to do as much as she could in the least amount of time possible during the coolest part of a summer day. Working furiously, she felt a pull and a tear in her arm. The next day, her arm hurt, and she had trouble moving it. Still, she went to work and even with the pain was able to complete her shift.

During that same weekend, Reb had also given her parents a very precious gift.

*   *   *

On the very day months before when Reb had forced her very ill mother to go to the hospital, her parents had lost a cat that they had had for many years, a special Persian cat that Reb had given them thirteen years before. The death of Tyson, her parents' tiny yet feisty flame point Persian, was absolutely devastating and at the worst of times considering her mother's condition.

Reb's mother had been ill for months, part physical and part mental. Her mother was extremely difficult to deal with, confused, paranoid, forgetful, and suffering from one infection after another with the so-called cure for each infection leading to the next. It was an extremely trying time for Reb but even more so for her father. Each time Reb and Sammy called an ambulance, Sammy would be left to deal with his father's tears, and Reb would be left to deal with everything her mother's condition entailed. On this true day from hell, Sammy buried the cat.

Eventually, many months later when her mother improved, her mother would have little memory of the time. For Reb, Sammy, and her father, however, it was a tough time. Thank God. Things eventually did get better.

*   *   *

Reb loved cats, and she particularly loved her Persians. She had one very beloved and very large and gorgeous cross-eyed, blue-eyed white Persian that was not getting along well with the other older cats that were in her home. She knew that this beautiful cat would be perfect for her parents, and so months later, after her mother was home again and able to take care of herself, Reb offered her favorite Persian to them. The day after Reb first injured her arm, her father came to take her precious Persian to his home.

Three days later, after being called by her parents that the cat was not doing well, Reb went over to help. Indeed, her favorite Persian was petrified by the change and was hiding. Reb called him, Gabby was his name, and she spotted him behind the couch in her parents' spare room. When Gabby wouldn't come out, Reb reached over behind the couch and picked her baby up. Gabby was a big and heavy cat. Reb felt her arm tear again. At that point, the arm was in agony, and she was unable to move it.

Over the next few hours, she felt numbness and could not move the fingers of her left hand in order to type. That night, she couldn't sleep as the pain was excruciating. She couldn't undress or dress herself. The next day, she couldn't shower. The pain got worse and worse.

She was as helpless as she had ever been.

Reb notified her employer of what had happened and that she could not work which, of course, as was typical of the company that she worked for, was not well received.

The next day, her brother took her to the hospital emergency room where they put the arm in a sling, prescribed a pain medication so she could sleep, and told her that she had to go to her primary care provider in order to have an MRI ordered. The next day, Reb went to her primary care provider who was sure that it was only a sprain but ordered the MRI anyway. Reb had the MRI a week later. Four days after that, her primary care doctor called to say that she had a severely torn rotator cuff with internal bleeding and that she would probably need surgery, but it was possible that she might be able to avoid surgery by trying a course of physical therapy while the arm healed. Reb elected to try the physical therapy.

*   *   *

Reb's injury took her out of work. No work, no income from Reb, and she and her husband had already been under great financial strain. Her husband had done everything he could to bring in enough money. He was now the major wage earner and worked long, long hours, yet they were barely making it. Reb's income as an entry-level MT was low, especially when compared with what she used to earn as a seasoned teacher. The company that Reb worked for was a fair one but had responded to the current recession by cutting the pay of the very people who brought in the revenue, typical of the times and shortsighted. Reb's pay had been cut by nearly a third. Now that she was injured, she couldn't bring in any income at all. Now that she was injured, she couldn't drive, and she couldn't take care of the people who needed her.

*   *   *

Reb and her husband had worked so hard and tried so hard. They were good people, proud people, independent people who asked little other than to keep what they had worked so hard for and be able to help the people who needed them. This just wasn't fair. Now, Reb was truly out of commission and what she and her husband had worked so hard for was truly in jeopardy. For Reb, this was the last straw. She became very depressed.

*   *   *

It was at this point, three days before her fifty-first birthday, that Reb just didn't want to do it anymore. She felt like a failure in every way possible. She couldn't earn an income. She couldn't clean her house. She couldn't even wash her hair or take a shower without help. She was letting her husband down. She was letting her family down. No matter how much she tried or how much she wanted it all to be different, she was helpless, and she hated herself for that.

At all other times in her life, whether because of the things that were done to her or the mistakes she had made herself, Reb had somehow found the strength to fight and come back to try again. But now, she could do very, very little. She was tired of the harsh realities. She was tired of everything going wrong. This time, she no longer had the energy or the will. She was completely exhausted and just couldn't find the strength to go on anymore.

Reb had had it and was ready to leave the world. She was exhausted. She had lost all hope. She was totally stripped. She was despondent, feeling helpless, and truly didn't care if she died. There was a part of her that was just plain pissed off, but mostly, she just felt defeated, sad, and hopeless. Her faith in God would never allow her to take her own life, and she had never entertained the thought, but she was ready to go anyway and simply had nothing left to give.

*   *   *

Reb had been thinking how much different her life would be if the early years of her life had been different, if she were stronger, smarter, and hadn't lost so much for reasons that hadn't been her fault or in any way in her control, if she had just made better choices. She wondered what life would have been if she could turn back time, knowing what she knew and do it all over again.

Knowing what she knew, she would have to go back a long way, years before she started smoking, years before she was involved with the wrong crowd, at least before she was five.

That night, Reb spoke to God with an absolute honesty that stripped everything away, any pretense, any denial, any hope. "God, I'm not worthy. For whatever reason, I'm not worthy. Let this nightmare end. I'm sick. I'm injured, and I'm tired. I keep trying, but something always happens to hurt me. I just don't want to do it anymore. If I had been smarter, better, maybe things would have been different. Please, either take me away or give me the chance to do it all over again. Maybe, just maybe, I would do better the second time around."

With that, Reb went to bed with a tear-stained face, a body in pain, not caring whether she lived or died and yet still, somewhere down deep in her soul, with a glimmer of a prayer.

*   *   *

REBECCA

She woke up with bright sunlight in the room, strange because she always kept the shades down and the curtains closed. She looked up and saw a roof, not a ceiling but a roof, a roof with metal springs and a mattress hanging down. It was a bed, a bunk bed above her. She stretched. She looked at her hands, then her arms. What? These were not her arms. These were not her hands. These hands were a lot smaller than hers. These arms were tiny. She was small but not this small, yet the arms and the hands were attached to her.

Next, a noise, someone jumping off the place above her and onto the floor. "Time to get up."

The floor, this wasn't her floor. It was hard and tiled, dirty old tile. Her bedroom had soft green carpeting.

Her bed didn't have a roof of springs above it. Her bed was bigger than this. Her bed didn't have anything above it at all.

The person standing on the floor was familiar, but he wasn't her husband.

The person standing next to her bed was her brother, a smaller version of her brother, healthy and young, maybe seven or eight years old, but it was her brother. She jumped out of bed.

"Oh my God what the hell?"

She was in a large room that she remembered well. It was long and rectangular with a hard floor that looked like tile but wasn't. She saw the bunk beds. She saw her bureau, a white dresser with a mirror that she had gotten rid of years ago. She saw her brother's chest of drawers that he had long converted to garage furniture. She saw a box filled with dolls, Lincoln Logs and toys and the Barbie case that she had long since given away. She saw another box filled with Tonka trucks, a couple of baseball bats, a ball glove, matchbox cars and games.

By this time, her brother had left the room to do whatever he was going to do.

She ran to the mirror and looked. This wasn't her. It was her, but it wasn't. This was a little girl, a very tiny little girl with short pixie brown hair, bright green eyes and no lines or ugly red veins. This little girl looked like she was about three feet tall. She had arms no wider than a ruler and no bigger around than a toilet paper tube. Her legs were equally skinny with the knobby knees that she had hated as a child. She had a flat chest, no waist and no hips.

This couldn't be her, but it was the image staring back at her from the mirror. The body that she saw in the mirror was the same one that her fingers touched.

"Okay, this can't be what I think it is. I'm dreaming. I'm hallucinating. Maybe I died and went to hell. Okay, calm down. This just can't be. When you leave this room, you are not going to see what you think you're going to see."

She looked down. She was wearing pink and white flowered flannel pajamas. She looked around for a robe but didn't see one. She looked by the bunk bed and saw a pair of very small ratty white bunny slippers. She put them on. They fit.

"Okay, what do I need to do now? If I'm where I think I am, I know what I'll see when I open that door." If she was where she thought she was, she was in one of the biggest rooms in the house. When she opened up that door, she would find herself in a long hallway. On the left would be an open door leading to a set of stairs going up to another floor. On the right would be a straight hallway leading to first another large bedroom and to the left of that a bathroom. In the bathroom would be an old claw bathtub with an iron sink with the pipes showing. Across from the bathroom would be another set of stairs leading to the downstairs.

She walked over to the door, opened it, and peered out. A long hallway, a door to the left leading up a flight of stairs, an open door at the end of the hall where she could see a neatly made double bed.

She wasn't even going to try going up the stairs to see what she knew would be there. She slowly and very quietly walked down the hall and looked in the room at the end of the hall. It was very familiar to her. In it were a double bed, two sets of dressers, and a television.

She had to be going out of her mind. She absolutely knew that she hadn't seen this in years, but there it was.

She moved over to the bathroom. It was exactly as she remembered. She heard voices coming from downstairs and turned around.

There were the straight gray wooden stairs that she knew would lead down to a very small front hall, a large wooden front door and to the left a small living room. In that living room would be a speckled brown couch made of a fabric that she could not name. To the left of the couch would be an old beaten-up brown La-Z-Boy, and in front of the couch would be an old coffee table made of a wood that she also didn't know the name of. About three feet across from the coffee table would be a console TV complete with rabbit ears and a dial channel changer.

Straight off the living room would be a large kitchen with a hard gray and white floor, an old gray and white spotted Formica table with six chairs, gray metal cabinets with a white Formica countertop and steel sink, a small white gas stove with four small burners, and a tiny oven and a small white refrigerator with rounded edges. Going straight through the kitchen would lead you to the backdoor and a small landing, four stairs, and a fairly good-sized backyard surrounded by a fence.

There would be an old apple tree in the very back of the yard, great for climbing, an area of dirt with Tonka trucks, matchbox cars, plastic shovel and marbles, and a large area of green grass to the left. When you turned left in the kitchen, you would come to another door leading to a set of rickety wooden stairs and a dirt cellar.

*   *   *

She turned from the bathroom and slowly and quietly made her way down the stairs. The voices she heard were much louder now. She turned to the left and looked through the door. There was the speckled brown couch. There was Tom Cat, her sister's large yellow and white patched cat, curled up asleep on the arm of the couch. There was the coffee table.

She walked through the door and turned to the left to see the old console TV with the rabbit ears. She then heard a voice that stopped her in her tracks. "Frosted Flakes, Lucky Charms, or Cheerios?"

*   *   *

She looked, and there she was, her mother, her beautiful, young mother. This was a lady with dark hair and a beautiful figure even if she was in curlers and an old house dress. This lady did not wear glasses, did not have gray hair, and did not walk with a walker, but this lady was her mother. This lady was moving around the kitchen, taking bowls out of the cupboard, taking a bottle of milk out of the refrigerator, taking spoons out of a drawer, and telling other voices to be patient.

Reb froze. This just couldn't be.

"Oh, there you are, honey. Got your bowl ready. Come sit at the table."

Reb walked through the doorway and froze again. There was her sister with her long brown hair in pigtails, no gray, much smaller and shorter, dressed in a sleeveless cotton shirt and stretch pants, sitting on one side of the table. She looked to be about ten or eleven. On the other side of the table was her youngest brother, Sammy, in checkered shorts, a short-sleeved cotton button up shirt and sneakers with a crew cut and looking healthy, certainly no more than six or seven.

At the end of the table, separated from the other two was the source of her worst nightmares, her oldest brother, Billy, tall, large, dressed in checkered shorts, a short-sleeved button up shirt, sneakers and glaring at her as she walked through the door.

Her mother gestured to the seat directly opposite from Billy.

*   *   *

Reb felt her panic build. "Okay, what do I do now? Do I tell them that I'm not who they think I am? I'm me but not the me that they think they see. Do I tell them that I'm not nuts, but I'm really fifty years old? Do I tell them that I know more about them than they could possibly imagine? Do I tell them that I know more about the world and that, yes, I can tell them what the future will hold? Do I tell them that I thought about a song that talked about turning back time, I prayed and now someone is playing a very sick joke on me?"

Reb did none of that. She just reached for the Lucky Charms.

*   *   *

"What year is it?" Everyone looked at her with surprise, certainly an odd question but even odder for a little girl who had barely started to speak in full sentences. "Why, sweetie, it's 1965." Reb swallowed hard but didn't feel like eating. "What month is it?" More surprise and more curiosity. This was really odd. "Why, honey, it's August."

"Okay, August of 1965." She was four years old. Oh my God, she was four years old! She hadn't even started school yet. "Okay, now what do I do? I'm four years old, but I'm not four years old. I'm fifty. But I'm not fifty. I'm four! I'm freaking out! I've got to get out of here. Think, think, think." Reb ate a couple of spoonfuls and said, "I got to go to the bathroom," and went upstairs.

She scrambled into her bedroom and flew onto her bed. Hiding under her covers, she thought, "What is going on here? This just can't be for real!" But it was. She had the body and appearance of a four-year-old. It was 1965 for God's sake! She was four years old! This had to be a dream, a nightmare, and if she pinched herself, she would wake up. She pinched herself and felt pain.

She knew that she wasn't on any kind of drug-induced trip. She had always hated the idea of drugs, could never take them, and had to be strongly convinced to take prescription medications that she really needed. No, she wasn't on drugs. She wasn't sleeping, she wasn't hallucinating, and she wasn't fifty. She was four!

"All right, so I'm four. But I remember so much. I remember everything. How can that be? In my heart and soul, I'm fifty; but in the mirror, I'm four. Everyone here sees me as four. So what the hell is going on?" Reb took a deep breath and then dared to believe.

"A 'do over.' You prayed for a 'do over.' God heard you, and he's giving you a 'do over,' a second chance."

Insane, yes, but what else could it be?

"Okay, so I'm being given a second chance, a chance to go back and change things, a chance not to be abused, broken, and squashed, a chance to be happy and do the things I would have done if it weren't for the abuse. Let me think. If this is what I think it is; it is God given. I have to do this right."

Reb thought long and hard. The more she thought about it, the more determined she was.

"It will be different this time. He's not going to get away with it. It's going to stop now, for all of us! I'm not going to be afraid anymore, not of him and not of anyone else. I'm going to be smarter this time, wiser, stronger. My family's life will be better. My life will be better. Billy, bring it on! This time I'm ready."

*   *   *

Reb got out of bed and sped down the stairs. Sammy was outside in the backyard playing in the dirt. Sissy left to go to the neighborhood pool with some friends. Billy was somewhere; she didn't know where. Her mother had cleaned up the breakfast dishes, dressed, done her hair, and was ready to walk downtown to go shopping with a neighbor.

"Becky, I'm going out for a while. Your brother is upstairs in his room if you need anything. Why don't you go outside and play with Sammy? I'll be back by lunch."

"Mom, would it be okay if you called me Rebecca? I like that name better."

Her mother paused, a little surprised but responded, "Sure, honey, I'll see you later, Rebecca. Have fun."

*   *   *

That was the first decision Reb made in her new life. She was and would be Rebecca, no nickname, just Rebecca. This time, she would be proud of the name she was given and never want to have it any other way. She was going to be a different person.

*   *   *

Rebecca went back upstairs. The first thing she did was go to her brother's toy box. In it were two bats, one metal, and one wood. She took out the metal one. It was made of aluminum and light. She could hold it easily, even in her very small hands. She waited. She knew what was going to happen.

In no time, she heard the footsteps coming down the stairs. She knew what they were and who it was. This was the reason why she first came back to this time, to this day. She had no memory of her childhood before she was four, but she remembered this, the first time she remembered being beaten. This time, she was ready, and she wasn't scared. She knew more than he did.

The bedroom door opened. "Mom's gone, you little bitch." And he charged. He didn't get far. With all her might, she swung. The bat hit him in the knees and he fell. Before he could shout out, the bat hit him between the legs, and he curled. Whining. Whimpering. Crying.

"Now, you slimy, rotten, stinking piece of shit, the next move I make is on your head, and I'll make damned sure it cracks open."

Rebecca hoped that God would forgive her for her language. Rebecca prayed that God would forgive her for her actions. He had sent her back to this time for a reason, and somehow, given the circumstances, she thought he would.

"Don't you ever touch me again. Don't come near me. Don't even try! If you do, I'll be ready, and you will never know how, but it will be worse than this bat. You might kill me, but I swear to God I'll do as much damage to you as I can, and if I'm dead, I will come back and haunt you."

"Don't ever touch Sissy or Sammy again either! Leave them alone, you rotten stinking bastard! If you touch them, if you do, I will find out. And leave Mom alone. You rotten stinking bastard, if you ever threaten or touch her again, I will get you. I will tell Dad. I will tell everyone. I will shout it out, scream it out, and yell until someone listens. I will tell everyone about the rotten things you do and will keep telling until someone listens and hauls you away. You're not going to get away with it!"

"And oh, by the way, if you try to tell anyone about this, no one will believe you, so don't bother, but you can try if you want."

While her brother was still writhing on the floor, Rebecca went over to the window and opened it just to make sure she might be heard if she needed to scream. She turned to her brother, walked over to stand above him, raised the bat, and said, "Get the hell out of here and don't ever come near me again." Her brother crawled out of the room, and she shut the door.

*　　*　　*

Wow! Did that feel good or what? Rebecca was elated. She was psyched. This was probably the best day of her life, both of her lives, but she wasn't a fool. She knew Billy's nature and would have to remain vigilant. Her brother would be pissed off and would never want to allow a little pixie like her to get the better of him. She was the main object of his jealousy, his hatred, and his perversion, and she knew the damage that he could do. At the same time, she knew that he wouldn't understand how his little sister could have said the things that she did or act the way that she had. He never would. No one would. That would be her edge.

She would be very careful, and no one would ever know. In this second chance, she would never allow her brother to get away with the things he had done to Reb, her mother, her sister, and her brother. Things would be different and better, but Rebecca was wise and knew that she could never tell anyone the truth, and she never did. This day was the first step.

*　　*　　*

Billy had disappeared, maybe up in his room, maybe not, but Rebecca was injury-free, and she wasn't scared. She was empowered.

It was time to go out to play. After all, what did four-year-olds like more than playing, except, in her case, being safe. So downstairs and out the door she went, out to the backyard where Sammy was playing their favorite play, marbles and building dirt roads for the matchbox cars. This would keep them busy until Mom came home from shopping to make their lunch.

*   *   *

That night, Rebecca experienced a time that she had long forgotten, a good memory that had long been buried because of so much bad, a regular night with everyone home. This was well before Billy's abuse would drive each of the kids out as soon as they were ready or able to leave, although with any luck, Rebecca had just changed that course.

In those early days, Rebecca's dad had held down at least one full-time job at all times and often had a second job on the side. His hours were long, sometimes erratic, and he would be away on nights, weekends or both. There were many times when her mother had to work hard to keep the kids quiet so that her father could catch a few hours of sleep. When her father was home, he was often working on the house. This very large house was her parents' first real estate, a very old apartment house that needed a lot of work. Her father was rarely available to his kids, and there were many times in those early years when her mother really was the only parent in her children's lives.

Her parents were poor but self-sufficient, hardworking, and doing the best that they could. They were products of the time.

Money was tight. The kids, with some exceptions, wore hand-me-downs from older cousins. Food was simple, required to be eaten no matter what was on the plate and on a predictable schedule of meals including Wednesday spaghetti night, Friday fish, and Saturday night beans and hot dogs. Of course, Reb had been an extremely finicky eater, so much so that the sternest command to eat something would end up with her throwing up on the table, so she became the exception to the rule.

Family vacations did not happen, although fun days away from the house would happen once in a while, and of course, there would always be the frequent trips to her grandparents' house.

*   *   *

On this evening, her first night as Rebecca, her father did come home from work, and they had dinner together as a family. It must have been a Wednesday because it was spaghetti, corn and, salad, most of which Reb would never have eaten.

"Dad's home. Dinner."

Her mother busily served up the meal and then sat at the opposite end of the table from her husband.

*   *   *

When Rebecca first saw her father that evening, she was first stunned and then moved to the point of tears. Here was this father she so adored, young. She knew because of the year that he was thirty-five years old, and in Reb's book, that was young. Jet black hair, no gray, no stoop to his posture, not thin, before most of the health problems; not the eight-one-year-old man that she had been looking out for for so many years. This was her father in his prime, the time in his life that he often reflected on with a glint in his eye. There he was, sitting across from her mother, her beautiful mother in her prime with dark hair, a beautiful face, no glasses, no stoop to her posture, a beautiful figure dressed in a pale blue dress and high heels. When Rebecca looked at her father, she saw that special sparkle in his eyes when he looked at her mother. It was a lifelong sparkle that would last more than sixty years.

Seeing her young parents together after so much time was almost Rebecca's undoing. The tears welled and began to spill. "What's wrong, honey? Don't worry, you don't have to have any sauce or salad."

Rebecca gathered herself and dried the tears. She thought, "I'm not going to be like Reb was. I can't. But I still have to be careful. My family will get used to the changes that they see. Might as well start now. Anyway, this is a good change."

* * *

"Mom, it's okay. I just got something in my eye. Can I try the sauce and a little salad?" They all looked at her as if she'd grown two heads. Sammy, Sissy, Billy, and her dad held their forks in the air and looked at her with expressions of shock and in Billy's case, suspicion. Rebecca knew that they had a reason to be surprised. Still, she knew that the change in her would have to start with this.

*   *   *

Reb had been an extremely picky eater, so much so that her mother had to prepare a side meal for her a lot of the time. Her parents had tried to be stern with her and make her eat whatever the rest of the family was eating, but it never worked. Whenever they tried to make her eat something she did not like or want, she would throw up on the table. She didn't do it on purpose. She just hated the food. It didn't happen too many times before her parents realized that forcing her to eat what she didn't want wasn't going to work. Reb hated all vegetables except corn on the cob and potato. She hated salad vegetables and salad dressings. She hated sauces, ketchup, mustard, mayonnaise. She hated all fruits except apples, strawberries, and blueberries. She hated all seafood except certain kinds of fish. She hated most meats except chicken, hamburger, and hotdogs. She hated white milk and eggs. She wouldn't eat anything like casseroles where foods were mixed together. She even hated MacDonald's and pizza. Unlike Reb, her brothers and sister liked to try different foods and rarely objected to what was on the table.

In later years, once an adult, Reb would begin to change and would eventually love vegetables, most fruits, and meats and would in fact be less fussy than others in her family.

*   *   *

On this first night in 1965, sitting with her family at dinner, Reb was Rebecca, and she had the palate and diet of a fifty-year-old. The change had to start with this. Maybe, just maybe, this change would help her to be stronger this time.

"Are you sure, honey?"

"Yes, Mom, I'm sure. Let me try. Please."

So her mother poured spaghetti sauce on her plain spaghetti and gave her a scoop of salad and a scoop of corn, and while they all waited for the inevitable upchuck on the table, Rebecca ate every bite.

*   *   *

That next Saturday, Rebecca and her family took their monthly trip to the country where her grandparents, her mother's parents, lived. As a child, the trip had always seemed so long, and she hated the drive because she suffered from carsickness, something she would grow out of. As an adult, she would see it differently and realize that the drive really wasn't long at all, maybe thirty minutes at the most, fifteen minutes by Reb's driving standard; but in 1965, the roads were different, the cars were different, and Rebecca's dad was driving. Still, Rebecca was excited about the trip. She was going to see the grandmother she adored, go to a place she loved, and maybe have some very special chocolate cake and molasses cookies that she hadn't had in more than thirty years. Best of all, she could check out some things along the way, most notably her own home forty-five years younger. This would also be a real testament to her ability to play the part of the little girl she appeared to be yet hide what she knew. It would be a very interesting day.

*   *   *

Just as her own mother would be forty-five years later, in 1965, Rebecca's grandmother was the true matriarch of the family. She was respected and definitely feared by her daughters. Without exception, she was respected and adored by her grandchildren. Her husband did whatever she told him to do and looked to her for guidance. Even her sons-in-law would never dare to question her.

Whenever any of her grandchildren visited, they were greeted with smiles, hugs, places to explore, a good helping of homemade molasses cookies, and a very special chocolate cake that no one else but her grandmother could ever make. When she died, the recipes died with her.

Rebecca's grandmother was a staunch Baptist who ran a very strict household and never wavered in her rules or expectations of others. Her grandchildren didn't see this part of her because, like most grandmothers, she was much softer where they were concerned.

*   *   *

Rebecca's grandmother was also a bit of a renegade for her time. In the early 1900s, she had attended and graduated from the Farmington Teacher's College in Farmington, Maine, and would work outside the home teaching in one-room school houses and a local elementary school for more than forty years. In those days, most women did not work outside the home, much less make a career out of it; and if they did, they didn't marry and raise a family. Rebecca's grandmother did all that and became a real inspiration to her granddaughters. For Reb's mother and her aunts, inspiration was not the proper word for how they felt about their mother. Her daughters feared and respected their mother and took care of the house as good dutiful daughters of that time were taught to do. They also, without exception, got out early and married against their mother's wishes.

It would be the granddaughters, all the granddaughters, who would go on to earn college degrees and build careers outside of the home. None of them, however, would ever do it with the finesse and control that their grandmother had. But in August of 1965, that was yet to come.

*   *   *

On the way to her grandparents' house, Rebecca didn't experience any of the impatience or car sickness that she would have experienced the first time around. In contrast, she was very interested in the trip and watched with awe each step of the way, seeing things clearly while standing in the backseat of the car with no seatbelt. She was so tiny that she could stand up in the car without her head hitting the ceiling of the car.

In those days, seatbelts were not required, and small children like Rebecca commonly stood in the back of the car not because safety wasn't an issue but because it just wasn't a concern. Rebecca relished in the freedom of it.

On the way, Rebecca saw so many places that she knew so well—businesses, restaurants, and hotels that she knew would still be standing many, many years later. Many of the large homes she saw along the way were family homes that she knew would someday become lawyers, doctors, real estate, and dentist offices. The roads were also different, sometimes because the names had changed but mostly because roads she expected to have two lanes only had one and most without even yellow or white lines.

Rebecca was most interested in the town that Reb and her husband would buy a house in. As they traveled along Route 2, she saw so many fields that would later hold businesses and housing developments, later making this very small town into a suburb. When Rebecca passed by her future house, she was surprised to see that it looked very much like the house she and her husband would own except that there was more land around the house because the future road work that would take land away had not happened yet.

As they continued on, Rebecca saw the little ice cream place, one of the first that served soft-serve ice cream cones that her parents had often taken them to when they went to visit her grandparents. Rebecca knew that it would go through many changes in ownership yet still stand and later become a used car lot.

When they turned to travel the road that her grandparents lived on, Rebecca saw so many empty places, small and large fields that she knew would later be dotted with trailers, small and large homes. She passed by a farmhouse wondering who was living there and knowing who would. She passed by a place that she knew would hold a restaurant that would go bankrupt and then become a realtor's agency and then an apartment complex. They traveled by a farmhouse that would later be torn down by the town because the taxes hadn't been paid. They traveled by a small cemetery that would remain exactly the same.

Rebecca was overwhelmed by the trip, by what she saw, what she knew, and what she couldn't say. She recognized that the changes that would happen were part of life and normal, but she had a tough time knowing what she knew yet being able to tell no one.

*   *   *

Rebecca's grandparents lived in a white farmhouse in which the original part of the house had been built in 1841 by her great-great-great-grandfather. Over many years, it would grow to include a large front porch, a large kitchen complete with wood stove, a good-sized pantry, a large living room, two bedrooms on the first floor, and three bedrooms on the second. In the mid-1920s, electricity would be added and by the 1940s, plumbing as well. Attached to the house was a large two-storied shed. In this shed, her grandparents stored and saved everything they ever bought: decades of newspapers, books and magazines, family picture albums, and the like. In years to come, it would be torn down and its contents, the stuff of dreams, to various antique dealers.

Behind and to the left of the house was a huge building that was referred to as the granary and had once held chickens. Near the road was a one-car garage. For the grandchildren, the chicken house was the place to be not because it held chickens; that had ceased before her mother was born, but because it was a huge place with huge rooms, lots of old furniture, clothes, and more books and magazines and was a great place to explore and build forts. Rebecca knew that it would be torn down by the late 1970s, but when she saw it on this August, Saturday in 1965, she silently greeted it like an old friend. It held fun and good memories and some of the few innocent times that she had had.

Turning into the driveway, Rebecca looked at the house with a feeling of great excitement and comfort. She knew that it would change little over the years. The shed would be torn down in the late 1980s. The house would be sided with some of the first aluminum siding during the time when they didn't remove the asbestos before they put the siding on, but aside from that, it really wouldn't change a whole lot. Inside, the house was full of treasures that were precious to each of the grandchildren, each for their own reason, and some that they would later inherit. In later years, it was one of the few things that Rebecca and Sissy would agree on, that it had been a magical safe place and that their grandmother had been one of the saving graces of their young lives.

*   *   *

Rebecca had forgotten that in those days, each and every time that her family visited, as soon as the car drove in the driveway, her grandmother would be standing in the doorway with a big smile and open arms. When the car stopped, the others scrambled out of the car, hugged their grandmother, and ran into the house to find the goodies. Rebecca got out of the car with her mother and father, timidly walked behind them, and stopped dead in her tracks. She was paralyzed. She tried but just couldn't help it. The tears began to flow.

Rebecca adored and revered her grandmother. She was one of the few people in Rebecca's life that could be trusted. Rebecca's grandfather was always there too but in fact was a pretty drab and dreary person who rarely showed any personality. Her grandfather rarely spoke or smiled. Reb was simply too young to understand that given her grandmother's strength and leadership, her grandfather really was the typical henpecked husband of that time and had long given up. When her grandmother died, her grandfather was lost and lived out the remainder of his days waiting to join her.

Rebecca was the youngest of the grandchildren and therefore the most spoiled, probably one more thing that Billy hated about her. While grandsons were loved, granddaughters were much more preferred and were doted on. There were five granddaughters in all, and they would all grow up adoring their grandmother and learning from her example.

When Rebecca saw her grandmother standing in the doorway, she was paralyzed. She couldn't help it. The tears just fell, not because she was seeing her grandmother again for the first time in so long, not because she was overwhelmed by being in this place that held so many special, comforting, and safe memories, not even because she knew that she would have her grandmother's special molasses cookies and chocolate cake again, but because she knew when and how her grandmother would die. This was the grandmother that she had loved so much and that she would mourn for deeply for many years. This was also one of the unforeseen prices of her "do over," the knowledge of what would happen to people that she loved, especially when their lives would be over, and Rebecca could tell no one. It was the first time she realized that this second chance would have its consequences and would also be lonely. Then she thought about her grandmother's example and was even more determined to succeed.

*   *   *

There was Rebecca's grandmother standing in the doorway, tall, statuesque, sturdy with curly gray hair, gray cats-eyed glasses, typical cotton dress, and sensible black shoes. Neither Sissy or Rebecca could ever remember a time when their grandmother looked anything but grandmotherly. Rebecca had seen photographs of her grandmother when she was young, and in her opinion, her grandmother looked better now.

*   *   *

"What's wrong, honey?" her mother asked. Rebecca remembered that in everyone else's eyes, she was just a little girl, a very little girl. "My tummy hurts. I think I gotta go to the bathroom." So she walked with her mother, gave her grandmother a quick hug, and headed for the bathroom. Once in the bathroom with the doors closed, Rebecca really was sick. She was on overload and her body was not happy. Maybe it was her body's way of slowing her down so she could cope. In any case, a few minutes later, she was able to walk out with her mother and face the family, the entire family.

Walking out the bathroom, Rebecca knew that she was in her grandfather's bedroom. It had a double bed, a bureau, and a drop leaf secretarial desk that she had always been fascinated by and would each and every time carefully inspect. Each time Reb visited her grandparents, she was drawn to this particular piece of furniture. She didn't know why. She just was. On the shelves were a mixture of

Bibles, historical books, and school books. Many, many years later, Reb would acquire the desk through a passionate argument with her aunt. She would have it refinished and fill it with her grandmother's books. It would be one of her most prized possessions.

Just outside of her grandfather's bedroom was the living room, a narrow, long room with a unique and intricate tin ceiling, the familiar large couch, her grandfather's easy chair, her grandmother's rocking chair, and her grandmother's piano complete with old-fashioned hollow piano bench filled with sheet music. At this very special piano, her grandmother would often sit with one or another of her grandchildren picking away at various tunes. Rebecca's sister would be the one most moved by this and would eventually inherit the piano, one of her most prized possessions.

Turning to the right of the living room, you would come upon the stairs to the second floor. The second floor had three bedrooms, one large and two small. It had been built in the 1920s but never used for bedrooms. Her mother and her mother's sisters had not had these rooms as their own. Rebecca's grandmother was deeply afraid of a house fire and would never let her girls sleep upstairs. Instead, all three girls slept in the other downstairs bedroom that would later become Rebecca's grandmother's room. In later years, however, when smoke detectors had been invented and the grandchildren came to stay the night, it would be one of these rooms that they would sleep in, usually one of the smaller bedrooms. This included Rebecca and was the only thing that gave her the creeps about her grandparents' house. She would later figure out that those bedrooms were almost identical in size and shape to her brother Billy's bedroom, complete with slanted ceiling.

The largest bedroom was very spacious and was never used. Even so, the room was very interesting because in it were very old dolls and baby carriages, antique furniture, old lace doilies, old clothes, and many other pieces handed down from her ancestors. Rebecca was nearly as drawn to this room as she was to the desk and over the years would explore it often, always avoiding the other two bedrooms that gave her the creeps.

From the bottom of the stairs when you turned right, you would see the larger downstairs bedroom, the one that her mother and aunts had called their own when they were growing up but was now her grandmother's room. The bathroom was actually between the two bedrooms and therefore had two doors.

Turning around, walking through the living room, and going through another door would lead to a large kitchen. This kitchen was very typical of its times. The cabinets were white and made of metal, the countertop made of Formica, just like in Rebecca's home but in much better condition. The floor was covered with red brick linoleum. There was a large woodstove and a small stove. The table was very old, very large, tall and with high-back chairs made of oak. Right off the kitchen was a large pantry where the refrigerator was with the trash can and more cabinets, these made of wood and painted white. Rebecca knew that in the years to come, this would change very little. Other than the wallpaper and the floor, everything else would stay the same. Even the table and chairs would survive and still be there when Rebecca was fifty.

*   *   *

On the oak table in the kitchen was the usual spread of cold cuts, lettuce, cheese, bread, mustard, mayonnaise, sliced cucumber, and tomato. Much more important were the molasses cookies and the wonderful, never-to-be-duplicated chocolate cake. Normally, Reb would have paid slight homage to the ham, cheese, and bread with absolutely no vegetables, no mustard, and no mayonnaise. With little of the healthy stuff, Reb would usually plow into the cookies and the cake. Rebecca knew why. No one, not one member of her family, would ever be able to duplicate the cookies or the cake. If they had, they would have made millions on the recipes.

This time, however, Rebecca would shock everyone there. She would ask her mother to make her half a sandwich, one with ham, salami, cheese, lettuce, tomato, and mustard. Again, her family would look at her in shock, and this time, so would her grandmother. So be it. This was one of the new things that her family would have to learn to accept.

Rebecca, tiny, forty-pound Rebecca, ate her sandwich and then devoured a cookie and a piece of cake. All her mother could think was "where does she put it all, and what is going on?" Her mother also thought, "Thank God." Most of her family looked at Rebecca and were shocked by the change in her behavior but still saw a tiny four-year-old with innocent green eyes. Her grandmother looked into those same eyes and saw wisdom. She couldn't put her finger on it but knew that there was something much different than just her granddaughter's eating habits. Her granddaughter was different, not only different from the rest but different from the child she had seen just two short weeks ago. Rebecca's grandmother would never know just how right she was.

In time, the family, even her grandmother, would get used to the changes in Rebecca and would come to see them as normal for her, but it would take time, and Rebecca would endure many more shocked reactions and suspicious looks, especially from her brother.

*　　*　　*

After a couple of more hours with their grandparents, the family packed up and headed out to visit her mother's oldest sister and brother-in-law, Rebecca's favorite aunt and uncle. They lived about five miles away in the next town over in a huge farmhouse complete with an enormous barn and a great yard with apple and pear trees, rope and tire swings, and a huge field. Her aunt and uncle had four kids, three who lived at home. The oldest, and also the oldest grandchild, was grown and in college. Timmy was Rebecca's age and always her favorite playmate when she visited. Her cousin, Natalie, was her sister's age and would later be Reb's singing partner in church duets. She would also become Reb's closest cousin and a good friend. In the 1990s, Reb would have Natalie's children in her Sunday school class, her junior church class and in the holiday plays that Reb would direct. Reb adored her cousin's kids and was pleased and proud as they grew into their adult years. But in 1965, Natalie, Sissy, and the oldest girl, Mary, were best buds and always took off together when the families got together.

When the family drove up the driveway, the kids quickly piled out of the car, Rebecca included. Before they could get near the house, the porch door opened, and there stood the large imposing figure of Rebecca's uncle, Uncle Jim. For the second time in one day, Rebecca stopped dead in her tracks. This time, she didn't cry, but she was overwhelmed.

Reb had never been particularly close to her uncle. He was always friendly and had a great bear of a laugh that Reb would giggle at. But he was also a little intimidating to her. She didn't know why. He just was.

In any case, for the second time in one day, Rebecca was faced with a person whom she knew was going to die. She knew the day and year that it would happen, and she knew why. It would be one of the first great unexpected tragedies for her extended family, not an accident or a crime but a fatal heart attack that could have been avoided with the right changes in lifestyle and the right medical care when the first symptoms occurred.

The problem was it wouldn't happen for many, many years. On this day in 1965, Rebecca was only four years old yet had the memories of Reb and knew what would happen. It didn't take much time for Rebecca to understand and know what to do.

This was her "do over." She didn't know if God meant it to be a "do over" for anyone else, but she knew that this was going to happen again and again and again. For now, it was 1965. She was four years old and there to visit and play with the cousins of her childhood in a wonderful old place that wouldn't stay in the family forever. She would just let what she knew of the future be for now and think about it later. Rebecca, Sammy, and Timmy took off for the barn.

*   *   *

Two weeks later, Rebecca started school for the second time in her life. This time would be different.

*   *   *

One of the few exceptions to her parents' strategy of saving money by clothing their kids in the extended-family hand-me-downs was underwear, socks, tights, and a very few articles of new clothing for school, especially for the beginning of each school year. On this second first day of kindergarten, Rebecca's mother dressed her lovingly in a beautiful white cotton dress with light blue pinafore adorned with blue and white flowers, pretty little lacy white ankle socks, and shiny patent-leather black shoes. Like the little princess that all four-year-old little girls want to be, Rebecca pretended that she really was four years old and gave into the impulse to twirl and tap. On this day, she did feel like a princess.

*   *   *

In those days, the elementary schools in the city she lived in really were neighborhood schools and didn't have buses, at least not until you went to junior high or high school. So on that first day of school, Rebecca happily walked to school hand in hand with her mother. The others had already left on their bikes.

The Birch Street School was a huge brick building that even at Rebecca's age of fifty, yet four-year-old eyes looked like a giant red castle. It had been built in 1888 and was even by the standards in 1965—old. It stood behind one of the neighborhood parks as an imposing building with a mountain of cement stairs just to enter the building. The front doors were huge and heavy, not something that a four-year-old could ever open on her own, even a strong one. Upon entering the building, you would see many classrooms on each side of the hallway starting with the second grade and going to the back of the school where the kindergarten classrooms were held. The third-, fourth-, fifth-, and sixth-grade classrooms were on the second floor. It was every kid's delight when they would reach the front of the second floor because that was the sixth grade and meant that they would be moving on. There was a music room in the basement and a small gymnasium. In those days and in that school, there was no cafeteria as lunchtime was an hour long, and everyone was sent home for lunch.

On this early September day in 1965, Rebecca walked down the long hallway to her first classroom. This time, she wasn't scared. She knew what would be there, who would be there, and what would happen; but this time, things were going to change.

Rebecca was only four when she started school, the youngest one there. She wouldn't turn five until the end of September, just a couple of weeks before the legal cutoff when she would have had to wait another year.

The first time she started school, Reb was the youngest, the smallest, and came from one of the more impoverished families in the neighborhood. She had spent the first years of her life protected by her mother and almost never exposed to children outside of her cousins and a couple of the neighborhood kids. She had had almost no exposure to the things that other children her age had experienced. She knew no letters, no numbers, no colors and could not recognize her printed name. She was confused by the language that people used in school and often did not understand what she heard or saw. Most of all, she was petrified. Reb did very poorly in her first year of school.

By the end of her kindergarten year, Reb's teacher tried to convince her mother that Reb was probably mentally retarded, should be tested, held back, and sent to a school for children with special needs. Thankfully, Reb's mother didn't agree and demanded that Reb would be passed onto the first grade where things would turn around remarkably, at least academically speaking.

Both Reb and Rebecca's kindergarten teacher was an old bitty named Mrs. Blanch. Neither Reb nor Rebecca was lucky enough to get the good kindergarten teacher, Ms. Brown. Her brother, Sammy, had Ms. Brown two years earlier and had thrived. Ironically, Ms. Brown would later become Mrs. Patch and teach in the same school for the next thirty-two years. Years later, Reb would teach in the same building with her and would come to know her as one of the best teachers she would ever work with.

However, in 1965, neither Reb nor Rebecca would be lucky enough to have Ms. Brown. Instead, Rebecca was again stuck with Mrs. Blanch who was, in Rebecca's opinion, an old hag who was near the end of her career and clearly a teacher who only liked the perfect children. Reb definitely wasn't one of them and would be a target of Mrs. Blanch's disdain during her first time around in kindergarten. On this second time around, however, Rebecca knew that things would be different. She already had Mrs. Blanch's number. She knew how to be respectful and impress the old witch. Rebecca knew her letters, her numbers, and her colors. In fact, Rebecca could read at a college level. She loved to write and knew terminology that hadn't even been invented yet. If she wanted to, she could blow the old bitty right out of the water. However, Rebecca was wise. She knew that she couldn't show the truth, not the real truth. Rebecca wasn't a genius, and she didn't want to be labeled as such. She would play it wise and just show enough to keep herself at the top of the pack. Most of all, this time, she wouldn't be afraid of the other children, and she wouldn't allow herself to feel any sense of shame for her background. She knew what she wanted and what she didn't. Rebecca was on her way.

* * *

In the fall of 1965, just after Reb turned five, she broke her arm, really broke her arm. It would be casted for months and would not truly heal until the end of her kindergarten year. It was yet another thing that had stunted her progress and made her weaker than everyone else. She had fallen off a bike that had first been her cousin's, then her sister's, then hers. It was rickety, rusted, and had wobbly training wheels. Reb fell off the bike while riding down a hill unsupervised. The break was severe and very painful.

This time around, Rebecca stayed away from the bike. She let it sit in the shed and refused to go near it. After all, she knew how to ride a bike without training wheels. She wasn't a bit afraid of riding a bicycle, just afraid of this bike. She would wait and borrow her sister's new banana seat bike that she knew Sissy would be getting for Christmas. In any case, Rebecca would show that she could learn to ride a bike without training wheels. This time, she never broke her arm.

*   *   *

By the end of her kindergarten year, Rebecca was at the top of her class and was one of her teacher's favorite pupils. "She is such a good girl," prattled Mrs. Blanch to her mother at the spring parent-teacher conference. "She is so smart and will do very well in first grade." Rebecca had spent a delightful year not being afraid of her peers, not being confused by the language the adults used, not being afraid to show what she knew a kindergartener should know, and most of all, not feeling ashamed of her family's poverty. She had no problem looking everyone in the eye and feeling just as good as they thought they were.

*   *   *

Over the next few years, each year would be just as successful as the first. Rebecca would stay at the top of her class, always be respectful toward her elders, and look every one of her peers straight in the eye. She wasn't intimidated by the luckier ones, the bigger and more attractive ones, nor was she afraid of the bullies. She was friendly and kind to everyone no matter who they were. In time, she was respected by her peers who couldn't look down on a tiny, ill-dressed girl who refused to look down on herself. However, she never allowed herself to get really close to anyone and had no girlfriends that she could confide in. First of all, she didn't trust; and second of all, she didn't dare. For one thing, she knew the futures of some of the girls, and it bothered her that in so many instances, she couldn't warn them. Some may have deserved what life was going to give them, but others didn't, and Rebecca didn't like knowing what she knew. Most of all, Rebecca was on a mission. This second chance was for her, not them, and she wasn't going to screw this up.

There were years when her attitude and certainly her understanding were much different than it had been the first time around. Reb had had her favorite teachers and school years. The first time around in her third-grade year, Reb had a male teacher who at the time she idolized, Mr. Ego. At the time, he was young, talented, and had a great sense of humor, often performing hilarious stunts for his students. By the time Reb was in the third grade, she really was at the top of the class academically, but she was not treated as a teacher's pet. Reb was a quiet little wallflower who rarely said anything and always did just what she was told. In her third-grade class, the role of teacher's pet was always saved for the boys in the class. Still, Reb adored Mr. Ego and counted him as one of the best teachers she had ever had. Yet this was also the year in which Billy had molested her. She had long since been beaten up by him, but this was the year when he did his worst.

*   *   *

Many, many years later, as a teacher/therapist, Reb would work in the same school which in the future would be a different building on the same site and with the same name. In fact, Reb would work in this building for twenty-three years. For a good portion of those years, she would work with Mr. Ego.

The very first time Reb saw him as an adult and coworker, Mr. Ego comically crawled under a table once hearing that she was a former student. After all, it only pointed out his age and how quickly the years had passed.

It wasn't long after this first meeting that Mr. Ego talked about how he remembered her family but did not remember her. He vaguely remembered her sister and brother, Sammy. He did, however, remember her brother, Billy. What a smart and spirited young man he had been.

For years, Reb buried the anger she felt at Mr. Ego's selective memory and lack of intuition. She never let it show and would often be one of Mr. Ego's favorite teachers to shoot the breeze with, which usually meant him telling her about all his accomplishments. Reb was very glad when Mr. Ego finally retired.

*   *   *

So this time, in 1968, when Rebecca went through the third grade for the second time, she decided to have a little fun. This time, she wasn't a silent little wallflower, still little but not silent. She loved to talk and ask questions and did so, much to the annoyance of Mr. Ego. She never laughed when he played the piano and sang the funny songs. She didn't react when he sat on his desk and pulled his legs behind his neck. She didn't look at him with adoration and certainly never became his favorite student, but she did earn perfect marks; and while this couldn't be called revenge, it certainly was freeing.

Most of all, this time, the abuse never happened. Rebecca was getting healthier, and she had no broken bones.

*   *   *

In 1969, Rebecca entered the fourth grade. Her teacher was a wonderful lady by the name of Mrs. Olden, another person whom Reb would work with many years later, even if only briefly. Unlike Mr. Ego, Mrs. Olden would remain one of her favorite teachers. Rebecca remembered her first experience with Mrs. Olden as a very good one. Mrs. Olden was one of those rare teachers, at least in those days, who expected each of her students to do the best that they could regardless of where they came from. Rebecca's second time in the fourth grade was just as good as the first, and she continued to flourish.

In 1970, Rebecca entered the fifth grade, the pinnacle of the old Birch Street School as the sixth grade had been temporarily moved to another building. Her classroom was at the front of the building on the second floor. Rebecca's teacher was the oldest teacher in the building, even older than that old bitty, Mrs. Blanch. Her name was Mrs. Lane, and Rebecca loved her. Reb had loved her too. This time, however, it was Mrs. Lane who recognized Rebecca's talent in reading and especially for writing. Reb had had the same talents but was timid and always afraid that someone would make fun of her if she wrote about the things she really thought about or wrote so well that others would recognize it and make fun of her.

Rebecca wasn't so timid. She was still careful and never spoke or wrote about anything that she shouldn't know or hadn't happened yet, but she could write book reports and essays. She loved to write and wasn't afraid to show it. After all, even if the other kids did make fun of her, their opinion didn't matter. In a very short time, less than ten years, whatever the other kids said to her wouldn't matter, but following her dream would.

Mrs. Lane recognized that in Rebecca, she had a talented writer, maybe not a great writer, but there was talent there and time would tell. Most of all, Mrs. Lane saw in Rebecca the beginnings of a very good teacher. This little girl, smaller than the rest, poorer than most, and the youngest in her class had leadership qualities. For the remainder of Rebecca's fifth-grade year, she would often be placed in group activities where she could help students who were struggling. She was always kind and never allowed anyone to feel that they were stupid. She remembered what it was like to feel those feelings and never wanted to be the cause of anyone else's pain. As Rebecca learned to believe in herself, she learned acceptance of others, but she did not learn to trust.

* * *

Rebecca finished fifth grade in June of 1971. Soon after, the old Birch Street School was torn down. The new school, the one that Reb would work in for so many years, would be a sprawling, single-level building with an unusual architecture that in Reb's opinion would never equal the original.

In 1971, however, the demolition of the old school and building of the new school would displace a lot of students. For the sixth graders, it meant that they would be housed downtown at the old high school. For the kids in Rebecca's neighborhood, it also meant that they would be traveling to and from school by bus, something that none of them had ever experienced. Because the entire sixth-grade population was housed in this school, it also meant that Rebecca would be going to school with a lot of kids that she didn't know.

The sixth grade was also the grade when schools began placing students by ability. There were three levels: A, B, and C. The C's were the students who historically had poor grades and/or were special needs. The B's were the average kids, the students who generally made B's and C's. The A's were the high average to above average kids who generally earned either all A's and B's or straight A's. Within each level, there was a breakdown of low, middle, and top so that each level had at least three separate classrooms. To Reb's dismay, she landed in the top of the top.

This put her in a classroom with very few people she knew and with a lot of kids coming from wealthy homes. She was totally out of her element, and it would be and was a miserable year, the worst year of school that she could remember.

Rebecca was also placed at the top of the top, but unlike the first time, she relished it.

*   *   *

During her elementary school years, Rebecca's parents strongly encouraged their children to work hard. This was met with varying degrees of success. Each child was given an allowance based on behavior and chores. In Rebecca's case, both were always good, so she earned the weekly maximum beginning in the earliest years with a dime then a quarter and finally fifty cents. Unlike Reb, Rebecca saved every penny and by the age of ten was able to begin buying some of her own clothes, at least enough so that she would look more like the other kids.

*   *   *

So, in the fall of 1971, unlike Reb, Rebecca began her year at the top of the top in a new school surrounded by rich kids but this time dressed in new, contemporary clothes that didn't make her stand out. This time, she wasn't scared. This time, she wasn't intimidated; and while she didn't welcome friendship, she was friendly and accepted. By Rebecca's standard, this time, she had a great year, continued to flourish, and was ready to enter the next year in what in those years was junior high.

· ·

In those days, there was no such thing as middle school. In the city in which Rebecca lived, the schools were divided into elementary, junior high, and high school. Unlike today, the grades of junior high school were seventh, eighth and ninth with high school being tenth, eleventh, and twelfth. The junior high classes were divided into levels, much like they were in Rebecca's sixth-grade year with the exception that rather than having only one classroom, students went to a different classroom for each subject yet also had a homeroom. The levels for each grade were A, B, and C with the same top, middle, and bottom. Not surprisingly, Rebecca landed in 7A just as Reb had. The difference was that Rebecca relished it and had no plan or desire to be anyplace else. Reb had deliberately sabotaged herself to get out.

*　　*　　*

When Reb was in the sixth grade, she had been devastated by the experience. Surrounded by beautiful and wealthy kids, she had often been the object of ridicule and bullying. She had hated that year of school more than any other and would never experience a school year that she hated more. By the time she reached the seventh grade and was yet again placed in this type of class, she had had it and was ready to get out. By the time she was twelve, she had become enmeshed with a group of kids, both male and female, who came from backgrounds similar to her own. With these kids, she felt acceptance and was part of a group. It was also in this group that she would, with the help of her sister who wasn't part of the group, begin smoking cigarettes. With this group, Reb would raise quite a bit of hell from shoplifting to breaking and entering. She would also try marijuana and alcohol. At the time, she thought that it was great, and she was so good at the sneaky part of it that her parents never caught her. By the time Reb entered the seventh grade, she had no wish to be one of the smart kids. She wanted out of the smart class and very deliberately set out to sabotage herself. By the end of her seventh-grade year, she succeeded.

During Reb's seventh-grade year, she deliberately failed or did poorly in many of her classes, not all, just the ones she really hated, like math. For her eighth-grade year, Reb was placed in 8C, just where she wanted to be. During her eighth-grade year, Reb raised more hell than she ever had or ever would again. She had lots of boyfriends including a boy who would years later become her first husband. She skipped school and continued to party. Her bad behavior and the behavior of her friends often got her in trouble in school, especially with the English teacher and the art teacher. She and her best friend looked for ways to be horrible, and they were very good at it. When kept after school by their English teacher, Reb and her best friend opened the windows and threw out a bunch of text books when the teacher stepped out for a few minutes. In art, she and her best friend worked on a secret project whenever the teacher wasn't looking, carving "bull shit" signs in florescent lettering. They smoked in the bathroom stalls, played jokes on other kids, forged their parents' signatures, and skipped school often. Whether luckily or unfortunate, they were rarely caught and were never reported to their parents.

Thank God that it wasn't long before Reb's better nature and judgment took over again. By the time she was thirteen, she would recognize what this type of life was doing to her and would shed both the group and most of the behavior. By the time Reb entered the ninth grade, her grades were again on the rise; and once reaching high school, she would be back in at least some of the top classes. However, she would have a lifelong addiction to cigarette smoking, common and accepted at the time, but still an addiction that would plague her and something she would always regret.

*　　*　　*

Rebecca wasn't going to have the same problems. Rebecca had not been devastated by the sixth grade. Rebecca knew what Reb had done, and she wasn't going to make those mistakes again. When it came time to move onto the seventh grade, Rebecca was ready. She was going to do the best that she could, and if staying at the top wasn't popular with some, so be it. Rebecca had the maturity of a fifty-year-old and knew that being popular and well liked wasn't really important.

Rebecca was friendly but did not have people whom she considered to be friends, and she pointedly and very certainly did not have a best friend. She wasn't going to be part of that crowd or any crowd. Most of all, she was not going to start smoking, drinking, or anything else. She had a plan, and nothing and nobody was going to deter her from what she reminded herself was her second chance.

*　　*　　*

So Rebecca went on to the seventh grade, stayed at the top of her class, and did the same in both the eighth and ninth grades. Rebecca never started smoking cigarettes. She never tried marijuana or any other kind of drug. She never did any shoplifting, and she never skipped school. Most importantly, she never had a broken bone and was never sexually violated. She made it through those years entirely safe.

She also never had a childhood best friend.

*   *   *

As for Rebecca's brother, Sammy, and her sister, Sissy, there were some changes that were at least a bit different than the first time around. Rebecca had not prevented the abuse that Sissy had experienced at Billy's hands. That had happened before her time. Sissy, with her independent and renegade nature, would quit school just before graduation, go to school to get her diploma through night school, marry young, divorce, go on to college, and become a successful scientist and devoted wife and mother. Her brother, Sammy, after no longer living under the fear of his brother's threats and abuse, would go through his childhood and teenage years as a well-loved and very energetic person, the wildest of the bunch, smart, savvy, independent, and hardworking, going on to become an executive in the computer industry, traveling the world, marrying and divorcing, raising his sons, yet still being struck down by a devastating illness later in life.

*   *   *

As for Rebecca's brother, Billy, well, that was another story, much different from what Reb had experienced. After Rebecca's confrontation with him, it was quite a while before he would try anything with any member of his family. He was suspicious of Rebecca but could never put his finger on anything that he could talk about. From time to time, however, his hatred, resentment, and true nature couldn't help but come through, and he would try something threatening or violent. Whether it was directed toward her or not, Rebecca had a sixth sense about her brother and was always there to show him that he wouldn't get away with it. She kept the memory of the baseball bat keenly in Billy's memory and let him know again and again that she had no problem coming up with something even better if she needed to and that it didn't need to be a weapon.

In time, Billy gave up on trying to bully or abuse his family. Instead, he struck out with a vengeance toward the kids in school and around the neighborhood. He targeted any male who he perceived as weaker than himself and used any excuse to demonstrate his hatred. He also got into taking and selling drugs. His father tried many, many times to intervene, but none of his father's methods worked. Eventually, Billy hit the wrong kid at the wrong time; and with his history of dealing in drugs, he was arrested. His long history of violent and delinquent behavior landed him in reform school, removed him from his home where he would remain until he was eighteen years old.

Once eighteen and having earned his GED, Billy entered the army and went overseas where he met his first wife. After the stint in the army and upon returning to the U.S., Billy and his wife would have two children, but Billy was lazy and didn't want to work. Billy would abuse both his wife and children, and the marriage would end in divorce.

After the end of the marriage, Billy would again become involved in drug dealing and would eventually get caught and sent to prison. In prison, he would try to bully men who were much bigger and stronger than he was. These men were not at all impressed with Billy and were much bigger and tougher than he was. Billy was killed in prison.

*   *   *

When Billy died, Rebecca was still in her teens. Her parents and grandparents mourned the loss of their son and grandson, but they were the only ones. Rebecca never shed a tear, and she didn't think that Sissy or Sammy ever did either. Billy's death meant that he could never hurt another person. While he hadn't been able to commit the terror and atrocities that he had done during Reb's lifetime, he had done enough even this time around, and he would have done more. Most of all, Rebecca still had the memories from the first time around where Billy was never held accountable and was comforted that he had finally been held accountable this time around. The only thing that Rebecca regretted was that Billy's third son, the best of the three, would never be born.

*   *   *

In the fall of 1975, Rebecca entered high school, which in those days meant the tenth grade. By this time, her parents had purchased a single family home close to the old gray apartment house, and the family had been living there for about four years. Rebecca had her own room and so did Sammy. Her sister had married young and moved out of the house. Billy was in reform school. Her father now had a good-paying job with Monday through Friday, 8:00 a.m. to 4:00 p.m., so that he was home every night and was able to take more of a role in his family's life. The house was peaceful, secure, and safe. Rebecca was doing well and ready to move on to the next step in her "do over."

*　　*　　*

It was a great year to start high school, the year of the bicentennial. Her brother was slated to graduate in June 1976, and it would be a very memorable year. There were things that Rebecca knew would happen that year that would be some of the best times of her life. Some parts of it had to be done differently; she knew that, but she couldn't give up the wonderful times that would happen.

During her first year in high school, Reb hero worshiped her youngest brother. Sammy was one of the most popular kids in the school. He was involved in sports, theatre and was liked by everyone including all the teachers and the principal. He also liked to party and raise hell, but he never got caught. Sammy loved his little sister and allowed her to follow him around. He never belittled her or made her feel like she shouldn't be there. Reb went to parties, on sports trips, worked backstage for the plays her brother was in, and even went to the senior prom with a much older senior. It was the best of Reb's high school years.

Rebecca wanted to experience that wonderful year again. This time, she went to the parties but didn't party the way Reb would have. She did, however, have a great time, again, and proudly watched her brother graduate in 1976. After that, she was on her own.

*   *   *

From the very beginning of high school, Rebecca had a very different plan from what Reb had done. Rebecca had goals, and she knew that it all started with high school. One step led to another. Reb had gone with the college-bound track, but Rebecca was much more practical and knew what would work for her. Rebecca was going in a different direction. This time, nothing, and no one was going to derail her.

Rebecca was still going to college. She was determined to still be the first in her family to earn a master's degree, but this time, she knew what the end product would be, and there would be no big mistakes, certainly nothing that would send her off in a direction that she didn't want to go in. The problem was that to get there, she would have to challenge some of the established practices of the time. Students in those days were either on the college track, or they weren't. The requirements and course work for college-bound students were very specific as were the requirements and course work if you were on the business or blue-collar track. The college-bound track got you ready for college and made you literate in the eyes of society, but it wasn't practical and much of what you learned would never help you in real life. The business-bound track was practical and relevant to real life but was so cut and dry that it didn't teach you to look for and understand the things in life that were not black and white, nor did it lead you to be literate in a manner that society at that time approved.

Rebecca clearly saw that neither course had what she needed. What she needed was a combination of both, one that led her to be formally educated in the way that was honored by society but practical in the way that was useful for her future. Rebecca's first course selection contained a mixture of high school requirements, college requirements, and business courses with no electives. She didn't want the fun-fluff courses and convinced the administration that the business courses could be counted as fluff if that was what was needed. Starting in her junior year, she would be on a different career track from the one that Reb had taken.

Physically, while only slightly heavier, Rebecca was healthier and stronger than Reb had been. Rebecca had never smoked, drank, or done any kind of drug. She had long since shed her finicky eating habits and was eating a healthy diet long before it became the thing to do. She had grown to a height of five feet and five inches and was 115 pounds, in better shape than Reb had ever been, and while she wasn't curvaceous in the way that most of the other girls were, she wore her height, weight and figure without shame. Rebecca knew that the curvaceous girls, the ones who were popular because of their looks, were often the ones that would have many children and end up divorced, overweight, many on welfare, and most looking old before their time. Besides, Rebecca wasn't interested in attracting anybody. She had been there and done that the first time around. She had been burned and just wasn't interested in revisiting the pleasure.

Secondly, just like Reb, Rebecca had been working part-time jobs for a very long time, starting when she was twelve. It began with babysitting and once old enough with jobs in stores, fast-food restaurants, laundries and as a chamber maid in hotels. She continued to buy her own clothes yet saved every cent she could.

So, in her junior and senior years and well dressed, Rebecca took a combination of college-bound courses and business classes. She took typing, accounting, and business math along with higher-level algebra, geometry, English, sciences, and Spanish. During her senior year when other students left early for jobs because they had enough credits to graduate, as did she, Rebecca stayed in school and took every class she could. Even though she hadn't followed the classic college-bound curriculum, nevertheless, she took her PSATs and SATs and scored well, high enough to be accepted in college.

The one extracurricular course that Rebecca did take was chorus, this time beginning in her sophomore year. She loved to sing, had a pretty good voice, and saw this as her one outlet. While Rebecca had not willingly changed much that happened during her sophomore year, she very pointedly changed what would happen in her junior year.

*   *   *

When Reb was a junior in high school, she took chorus as one of her electives, something that she really loved. The high school chorus was large, and they would put on several performances throughout the year. When they did, the school orchestra would be part of it, and the two groups often worked together. It was here that she met a small, cute, good-natured blonde young violinist named Nick. Nick and Reb would also share a couple of classes together, and she would find herself tutoring him so that he could pass the classes. In no time, Nick and Reb would become an item, and he would become her first real love and love him, she did, fiercely, so much so that she assumed that like her parents this first love would be the one for a lifetime. It would be forever. It wasn't. With Nick, Reb would hang out with yet another crowd that did things that were not good for her. They would be a couple for the rest of high school and into the first semester of college. He would tell her that he loved her and convince her to give something to him that was precious. Then he would betray her, and she would be utterly destroyed, her heart broken and not understanding that this was the way it happened to a lot of people and that her parents' young love and marriage was really a rare thing that would become even more rare as the years wore on. At the time, however, the pain she felt was devastating. She would get over it and move on, yet nothing about it would be a memory that she wanted to live with. It was a failure that hurt nearly as deeply as the abuse she had lived through in the years before.

This time, Rebecca could again change what would be. She could avoid the pain and devastation. This time, she wouldn't and didn't acknowledge Nick's existence. No one was ever going to hurt her like that again.

*   *   *

In June of 1978, at the age of seventeen, Rebecca graduated from high school, number 3 in her class and slated to begin college in the fall. By this time, she was the only one still living at home. Her sister was now divorced, in college, and living on her own. Her brother, Billy, was in prison. Her brother, Sammy, was in New Hampshire, married, the father of a baby boy, and was working for a new computer company, a company that Rebecca had invested in. Her parents had sold both the apartment house and the home that the family had lived in for the past seven years. On the day that Rebecca graduated, her parents moved into their new home in the country, and Rebecca stayed with them until it was time for her to go off to college. Again, this time things would be different.

*   *   *

This time, Rebecca had a very specific plan. She realized that the only real success in life was a plan that would make she and her family safe, and by safe, that meant money, lots of money. At the same time, Rebecca was going to follow her passion and somehow make the two work together. Rebecca's true passion wasn't that much different from Reb's, only this time around, it wasn't going to be sidetracked by circumstances that were not in her control.

Just like Reb, Rebecca was a born teacher, down to her very soul, but her goal wasn't to become a speech therapist or even a teacher of the deaf. It would be much more. Rebecca understood that teaching was not the wealthy woman's choice of vocation. It was a tough job that would never take Rebecca to where she needed to be to be safe, and safety was what she desired the most. Rebecca, however, had a plan and found a way to make the two worlds work together.

*   *   *

While in high school, Rebecca took business courses and read a lot about investment. Aside from her clothing expenses, she had saved quite a bit of money and began buying stocks. Rebecca had Reb's memories and knew so much about the future. Her memory of sports was hazy, especially during the 70s and 80s, so she knew that for her that that wasn't the way to go, but she did know what products were either new or hadn't been invented but would be. She knew what products were gold for investors, and she researched companies that sold those products. In the late 70s, Rebecca settled on a few products that she knew would be huge sellers in the 1980s: computers, the early days of PCs, microwaves, electronics. She knew that Microsoft was already in the works but had yet to explode on the scene, the same with Apple. Rebecca researched and found out how to invest using her meager savings. As those early investments began to earn dividends, she reinvested until she had built a small portfolio. Throughout her college years, she resisted the temptation to use any of the money for her college expenses. Instead, she took out student loans and worked at a variety of work-study and other part-time jobs, full-time during the summer.

Just as Reb had done, Rebecca went to the University of Maine at Farmington. This time, however, she majored in early childhood development and elementary education. This time, she didn't go home on the weekends but stayed on campus, studied, and worked part-time at a store in the area, going home only for semester breaks. This time, she didn't leave the college to get married and never met Reb's first husband. Like Reb, she did purchase her first car, but it was in better condition than the one Reb had purchased.

The course of study that Rebecca chose was much easier than the speech pathology major that Reb had been mistakenly led into. For the most part, Rebecca breezed through her first four years of college and graduated in 1982 with a bachelor's degree in early childhood development and elementary education.

*   *   *

In November of 1981, Rebecca's Uncle Jim died from a massive heart attack. Rebecca had long known that it was going to happen, just like she knew that John Lennon would be murdered by a crazy person; Ronald Reagan would be shot during his first term as President; Bill Clinton would cheat on his wife and lie about it; and September 11, 2001, would be the worst attack on the United States since Pearl Harbor. She knew when her grandmother was going to die, when her grandfather was going to die, that her sister would give birth to a beautiful little girl with many challenges in 1987, the same year that her father would become very sick from an unknown illness, that her mother would break her hip in 1997 rendering her challenged for the rest of her life, and that her precious youngest brother would be diagnosed with lupus.

Rebecca had long decided that telling people about these events in advance would be an exercise in futility and would mark her as a crazy person. She had to believe that she had been given this second chance to change her own life, not the world and not for much of what was destined to happen to her family. She was focused on her new future and wasn't going to be deterred.

Unlike Reb, when her uncle died, Rebecca was not nearby when it happened. Unlike Reb, she was not leaving a bad marriage. Unlike Reb, she did not move in with her aunt following the death of her uncle and the end of her own marriage, both of which happened on the same day, and unlike Reb, Rebecca would never form the very close relationship with her favorite aunt. It was one of the tradeoffs to her new life and one that she accepted.

*   *   *

In 1982, the University of Maine at Farmington did not have a graduate program. Rebecca wanted a master's degree, not only because, like Reb, she would be the first one to earn one but because she wanted the credentials for her future plans. So she applied and was accepted to the University of Maine at Orono and was accepted in a program that would allow her to again have a dual major, early childhood development and elementary education. This time, Rebecca would use her student loans to help her stay in the dorms and would continue to work in work-study and part-time jobs. What she would not and did not do was to work in the jobs that Reb had worked in, particularly the one that Reb was working in when she became a single mother. This time, Rebecca never met the man, and she never became pregnant. One more disaster averted, or so she thought.

In 1984, Rebecca graduated with a master's degree in early childhood development and elementary education. She was quickly hired as a preschool teacher in a local preschool for very low pay. She didn't care. She loved the work, loved the kids, and attacked the job with great relish and joy. After all, she knew that this job was only temporary. Rebecca had plans, and they were about to come to fruition.

*   *   *

Long ago, Rebecca had decided exactly what she wanted to do. She was going to build a preschool of her own, not just one preschool but a chain of schools that would be top of the line, preschools in more than one state, preschools that would cater to all levels of students from the most needy to the brightest. Rebecca would use Reb's knowledge of special education, speech therapy, occupational therapy, physical therapy, and the many categories of special education students that Reb had worked with for so many years to hire the right people and institute the best early education for those types of students. She would use her degrees in early childhood education and elementary education to convince others of her legitimacy and lead her to providing the best for all the average and above average students. Her preschools would be the brightest, the best, and the most desired. She had plans and methods for doing it all and would finance it by making her investments work for her and starting small.

In 1985, Rebecca used part of her investment returns, negotiated with the bank, and found the first building and grounds that would house her first preschool. In 1986, she opened "All Kids" preschool with a single classroom, herself as the preschool teacher and one assistant, at lower rates than the other preschools in the area and with herself and her assistant earning very low pay. She patented the logo for her preschool which was a string of connected paper dolls in different colors and sizes. During the first year, she didn't accept any severely handicapped students because she knew that this beginning business could not do them justice. She did, however, accept children with milder special needs, worked with her assistant to learn how to deal with them, and encouraged a lot of volunteering on the part of parents.

Her first year was very successful, and word quickly spread that hers was the new place to be. By the beginning of 1987, she was swamped with applications and expanded to two classrooms, hiring another preschool teacher and two more assistants. This year was equally successful, and by 1988, Rebecca raised tuition, expanded to three classrooms, and hired another teacher and another assistant. By the spring of 1989, her preschool had expanded to its limit, and Rebecca knew that the next step would be to add another school building, in a different place of course.

During the early years of building her preschool empire, Rebecca did a number of other things that were somewhat new during that time. First, she negotiated with state agencies to provide special therapy services and special instruction to the children she, parents, or the other teachers identified as needing it. In her preschool, she provided special spaces and materials and demanded that all the student's programs be individualized while still being part of the group, no matter what the background or the special needs. She worked hard behind the scenes in promoting an attitude and philosophy that advocated more help earlier in life when children were most able to learn. She even took this philosophy to the state level and spoke forcefully and loudly about giving these children more services early on when it would do the most good.

She also worked hard with parents and encouraged them to advocate for their children even when it was uncomfortable to do so. At the same time, Rebecca well remembered how much Reb had hated parents who bullied, screamed, yelled, and used the school as a platform to air their own bad experiences or their own agenda, which was often one and the same. Rebecca valued the parents of her students and felt that from the start, they needed to understand that the people dealing with their children were usually good people who did what they did because they wanted to help children, were not getting paid a lot for what they did, put in a lot of unpaid overtime, and didn't need the unwarranted nastiness, bullying, or hostility. Reb had been exposed to this type of treatment many times over the course of her career, as had her colleagues. In most cases, weak administrators had allowed it to happen and rarely did anything to control the errant parents' behavior. Most of the administrators Reb had worked with either didn't give a damn or let the parent have their way to placate them and thereby solve the situation for the moment. This wasn't going to be allowed in Rebecca's school. Rebecca demanded that all people, no matter what their background or role in her school, be treated with respect.

Rebecca knew that in her school, she and her employees were providing the best of the best, and she and her employees deserved to be respected and protected. In her preschool, if and when parents were hostile, Rebecca would warn them that their behavior was neither appropriate nor welcome, and if they didn't change, she gladly refunded their money and dismissed the students. She truly hated bullying.

Bullying wasn't confined to children. Rebecca also remembered the bullying that Reb had endured from certain staff members in the schools that she had worked at over the course of twenty-four years with one staff member in particular being allowed to get away with it for a very, very long time. Again, Reb had worked with weak administrators that excused the behavior and/or just didn't want to deal with it, allowing it to continue on and hurt many, many people, teachers, fellow staff members, parents, and yes, sometimes even students because of the fear instilled in them. In this, Rebecca was also adamant that she would not allow it in her workplace. She was very intuitive and careful in hiring each and every person in her preschool. She relied highly on her own instincts, and if she spotted any sign of an aggressive or bullying personality, that person never had a chance of being hired. Very rarely, her instincts didn't work, and she would hire a person who was by nature a bully. When she was told about their behavior and confirmed the signs of aggression, intimidation, or any other characteristic of bullying through her own observations, that person was fired right away. Yes, bullying wasn't confined to children, and Rebecca knew that it happened in every workplace in America, public and private, but it wasn't going to be allowed in her workplace. This time, she owned the workplace.

During the earlier years of building her preschool empire, Rebecca continued to invest, reinvest, and build her financial portfolio, especially in computers and electronics. Early on, she hired an accountant who helped her keep track of expenditures, income, and potential to expand. She avoided undue use of credit cards no matter how attractive the rates. Her bills were always paid, and she remained in the black.

During those early years, Rebecca also began working on the other project which she had thought of and planned on years before, Taylor Made.

*   *   *

When Reb was a young and inexperienced speech therapist, she found herself in a world that expected her to have a practical plan. Her college experience, even the practicum, had taught her more about theory than practice, and it took time to learn to put the theory to teaching that would result in her students making progress. She found the same thing to be true with new teachers in other disciplines. Therefore, in Rebecca's second chance came the idea of Taylor Made.

Taylor Made would ultimately be a series of how-to books, giving practical ideas and guidance for all types of students at all ages. There would be guidance that could be applied to each and every student individually. The first book would be a general book of activities that would apply to the preschool population and would include in it expected skills in development from the age of early infancy to age five. The book would be very specific and would include the materials required and references needed for all activities, including appropriate acknowledgement and legal permission when including any copyrighted activities. Developmental levels were provided at the back of the book and listed expected levels of performance in cognition, fine motor, gross motor, speech and language, self-help skills, feeding, social skills, and behavior. It was an ambitious project.

Rebecca couldn't do this one alone, and she realized it even before actually starting the project. As she gained a professional relationship with the other teachers and the various therapists who provided services in her preschool, she was able to put together a group of people who would work together to create the first book with everyone sharing a percentage of the profit, if the book was successful. Rebecca, of course, would receive the largest percentage, and she had already patented the name.

*   *   *

By 1991, the first book was ready for publication, only it was too large. Rebecca and her colleagues decided that it would have to published as a set of three; the first containing activities, the second containing the developmental levels, and the third containing specific ideas for a variety of special needs children.

In early 1992, the books were published: Taylor Made, Volumes I, II, and III, the Preschool Years. Within a year, the books were a success. Within two years, the books were a mega success, not just locally, not just statewide but nationally. Rebecca's books were listed in all the educational catalogues and became one of the most sought after references for early childhood education and preschools. When she realized what a success this was going to be, Rebecca formed a company, Taylor Made, Incorporated. She was becoming somewhat of a wealthy person.

In 1994, Taylor Made, Incorporated released their second set of manuals, this time for kindergarten, using the same format. As the company grew, manuals were periodically released for each grade level culminating in a book specializing in each of the major areas of special needs, including cerebral palsy, autism, and mental retardation. Over a span of twenty years, Rebecca's company would grow and grow and would employ hundreds of people. The one thing that Rebecca was adamant about was that the base company would always stay in Maine even if certain parts of it had to be outsourced to more urban areas.

* * *

Yet with all her best-laid plans and with all the success, there were some things that Rebecca could not control.

* * *

Starting in 1985, Rebecca began having visions, flashes of memories that just happened and were unstoppable. The first was of a tiny baby with bright green eyes, no hair, wearing light blue corduroy Oshkosh overalls, lying on a soft gray carpet with his little stocking feet sticking up in the air, his first professional photograph. Rebecca pushed the memory away.

Sometime in 1986, a vision of a baby, ten months old, blonde with bright green eyes, wearing a beautiful blue knit outfit, sitting in a rocking chair, his second professional photograph. Rebecca pushed the memory away.

In 1987, Rebecca dreamed about a toddler, a handsome blonde boy with bright green eyes wearing jeans and a blue and red sweatshirt that said, "I'm gonna win." Rebecca woke up with tears on her face and pushed the memory away.

Over the years, Rebecca would either dream or suddenly have visions of this little boy as he grew and changed from bald to blonde to darker hair and then the dark hair that she had, always with the same bright green eyes and beautiful smile, always with his infectious laugh ringing in her head, and eventually seeing him in the handsome uniform of a United States Marine.

Each time, she pushed the memory away.

*   *   *

By 2011, Rebecca was a very, very wealthy lady.

*   *   *

Before Taylor Made took off, Rebecca worked hard to expand her preschool. Once her first preschool was successful and solid, she moved to Portland and built a new preschool, the second of her "All Kids" schools. This time, she had the building and grounds built to her own specifications that would house four classrooms, small rooms for therapies, a gymnasium, and a large playground area. Once this preschool took off, she expanded into New Hampshire and Massachusetts and within fifteen years would have schools in all the New England States. In 2005, she sold the entire chain but insisted on a clause that would provide her with a percentage of the profits for years to come.

Between her investments, the sale of her preschool chain and "Taylor Made," by 2011, Rebecca was indeed a very, very wealthy lady.

Rebecca was so determined to be successful that she ignored the flashes of memory and pretended that it didn't matter. There was a cost that no amount of money could ever pay for, yet Rebecca just wasn't ready to face it.

*   *   *

During the years between 1984 and 2011, Rebecca was very busy. She had little if any time for family and had no time for friends, not that she was interested in having any. It didn't mean that she wasn't friendly. She was. She just never got close to or allowed anyone to get close to her. She had plans and an agenda and wouldn't allow anyone or anything to get in the way.

During the 1980s, Rebecca's being busy with her career wasn't a problem. In those years, her parents were still in good health and doing well. Her brother, Sammy, was at the top of his game. Her sister was remarried, had a child, had a good career, and was happy. Her brother, Billy, was dead, and no one talked about him, good riddance to human garbage as far as Rebecca was concerned.

When her grandmother died in late 1988, Rebecca was there to attend the funeral, but she didn't share the close relationship with her relatives that Reb had had. That was okay. After all, they didn't know the difference.

In 1992, Rebecca's grandfather died. Again, she went home to attend the funeral, and again, she was pleasantly appropriate to her immediate family and to her relatives. Her heart and mind were elsewhere.

By the mid-1990s, during the time her parents' health started to decline, particularly her father's, Rebecca was in great shape financially. During those years, Reb would have spent many hours caring for her father both in the hospital and at home as well as helping her mother. This would have been in addition to working more than a full-time job and taking care of her own home and family. Rebecca didn't have that problem. She was wealthy and could hire the help that her parents needed, which she did. Once her parent's health started to decline, she hired help in whatever way they needed: Nursing, cleaning, grounds keeping, transportation, even shopping, and dress-making for her mother when she needed it. Medically, financially, and materially, they would be taken care of for the rest of their lives.

In 2002, when her brother, Sammy, was diagnosed with lupus and could no longer work, Rebecca did the same thing. Whether he liked it or not, she paid off his house and made sure he had the best of medical care, such that it was, and would always have all his financial and material needs met. As with her parents, Rebecca hired help in whatever way she thought he needed: Nursing, cleaning, transportation, and even companionship. In this way, her brother was able to stay in the home that he loved in the place that he loved and would never have to go through bankruptcy as he had done in Reb's lifetime. Rebecca felt very good about this.

As her wealth grew, Rebecca was able to do things not only for her family but for causes that she truly believed in. She was generous with certain charities such as the Special Olympics and the Children's Miracle Network, but when she donated, she always donated anonymously.

Rebecca's most important charity was one that she herself began in 2005. It was different and was not created for either children or the poor.

In 2005, Rebecca anonymously started a program called "Middle Hope."

Before Reb retired from teaching, she and her husband were a part of the comfortable middle class, the ones who made enough money to have a mortgage, a couple of decent vehicles, decent clothes, and an occasional vacation away from home. When Reb was forced to retire early from teaching, the situation changed and finances became much more challenging even though, thanks to her husband's income, they remained in the middle class. It didn't take long, however, for Reb to become tired, frustrated, and fed up with how the middle class were treated in this country, some of the hardest working yet also the highest taxed and the last ones to get help when they not only needed it but had worked their asses off to earn it. Reb had worked in the schools for many, many years. She had worked as a medical transcriptionist in her second career. She had experienced and listened to so many cases about hardworking, middle-class people who lost the homes and livelihood that they had worked so long and so hard for because of unforeseen catastrophes, illnesses, or in most cases one and the same. When in need, the middle class almost never received the help that they needed.

From Reb's experience, the poor received so much support through welfare and other tax-paid services that most never even contributed to. So many of the poor that Reb had encountered in her life felt entitled to the handouts that society provided for them and didn't show any acknowledgment or understanding that there were working people paying the taxes so that they could have these services. Many of these people were also some of the most rude and arrogant people that she encountered.

The middle class, who paid the greatest amount of taxes and had worked hard for all their adult lives, couldn't rely on those same services when they needed it. The poor would qualify for full medical insurance at state expense and could receive whatever services they needed. The middle class had to pay a high premium for their health insurance or be under insured or not insured at all. Tax increases almost always hit the middle class the hardest. The poor didn't pay the taxes, and the rich either found ways to avoid taxes or were so wealthy that it didn't really hurt them anyway.

Both Reb and Rebecca felt very strongly that people should not be punished for getting sick, but it was much worse when hardworking, caring, responsible people lost everything that they had worked so hard for because of an illness or accident. In Reb's case, it was really personal because she had been there and was in danger of being there again. So had her brother.

"Middle Hope," started in 2005, was a nonprofit organization created to help those middle income people who had had a catastrophic event, whether it be accident or illness that threatened to take home and other hard-earned possessions away. The service was not given easily and certainly not to anyone who could not show a long work history. Applicants were put through a rigorous, careful, and confidential process that if accepted would result in their medical bills being paid, their mortgages and car payments being paid, and allotments for food and clothing. For clients with a hope of retraining, help was given to assist them with finding the next best steps, including a new career. For clients who were permanently disabled, their homes would be paid off, and they would be provided with an income until their disability income kicked in. In any case, no client who was accepted in the program would ever lose their home because of illness or accident. Ironically, for Rebecca, the entire program was tax deductible, one of the benefits of being wealthy.

*   *   *

By 2000, Rebecca was a wealthy person. By 2005, she was a very wealthy person. By 2011, Rebecca was a millionaire many, many times over, not to the level of

Oprah, but not too shabby for a kid who started out wearing hand-me-downs from the 1950s.

*   *   *

By 2011, Rebecca was healthy, strong, and rich. She had achieved everything that she had set out to do. Her family was safe and well cared for. She was safe. No catastrophe could touch her. Her second fifty years had been so much more successful than her first.

Over the years, she had not seen much of her family, going home only rarely for holidays and other special events. For years, she had lived in luxury apartments or condominiums with good security and no maintenance requirements that she had to do herself. Even though Reb had always had cats and loved them dearly, Rebecca had never had any pets. First of all, she didn't want to deal with the mess and responsibility, but most importantly, Rebecca didn't' want to go through the heartbreak every time a much loved pet was either killed or died from old age.

Rebecca hired professionals for her cleaning, cooking, shopping and transportation. She never dated and only welcomed male companionship, usually a coworker or business associate, when she needed an escort for a charitable event or a special invitation. She would never allow herself to be interested in a relationship with any of them. Rebecca knew that relationships were a lot of work and compromise and usually ended up in heartbreak. Rebecca wanted only to live with her own expectations, never a man's as Reb had done.

Rebecca did have many acquaintances and business partners but never anyone she considered to be a true friend. She remembered how often Reb had been hurt and knew that no one, not even her longest acquaintances, could ever really be trusted. She kept a low profile and didn't welcome publicity or public attention of any kind.

For all of the second fifty years, Rebecca was safe.

*   *   *

Three days before her fifty-first birthday, Rebecca took a rare day off. Sitting in the living room of her condominium with its beautiful professionally decorated décor, she took a long look at the last forty-seven years. She was proud of what she had done. She had changed her entire life and lived it in the only way that had made things right. Life had been good to her and to the many people that she cared for. Her family was safe and secure. She had never been sexually abused, and her bones were not broken or fractured. She had not allowed anyone to hurt her. She was safe and secure.

Yet, no matter how much she didn't want to face it, the ghost of Reb would creep in without warning. Admittedly, Rebecca was alone and lonely. She had long since learned to ignore the nagging sense that there was something wrong with her plan, and she had pushed away the memories that she did not want to face. The realization had been creeping up on her slowly, and no matter how hard she tried, the sense that she was missing something nagged at her subconscious and came into her dreams. In all the time that Rebecca had been working so hard, she had never bothered to or even wanted to take the time to think about anything that wouldn't move her forward with her plans. As she became more successful and most of all safe, loneliness began to intrude on her perfect world. At fifty, she couldn't help but think about the things she avoided voicing to herself. Most of all, she thought a lot about the person she had been before, Reb.

The problem was once she started, the thoughts wouldn't and couldn't be stopped. Reb had become very adept at keeping feelings in check. Rebecca had been much better at it, yet, like Reb, once the floodgates were open, there was no stopping it.

* * *

Rebecca had been afraid to make friends. Friends took work and often were not there when you needed them. When Reb had been hurt, so many times, there had been no friends to help or the friends that were part of her life at the time had somehow disappointed her or just not been there at all.

Rebecca had been afraid to fall in love. All the men that Reb had ever cared for had hurt her, just like her friends.

Rebecca had the memories from the age of four and was a natural pessimist who knew better than to trust. Reb was a born optimist and had tried to trust, had for many years believed that most people were good and cared like she did, but had painfully learned that, at least for her, trusting others was a dangerous thing.

Rebecca loved her family and felt obligated to take care of things. Reb had too, but Rebecca had been better prepared and found a way to do the right thing yet not have it interfere with her life.

Reb had spent much of her adult life caring for everyone but herself. Rebecca had found a way to do the same thing but with little personal involvement or obligation.

As the years went by, Reb had spent more and more time with her family. She loved her family dearly, save one, and over time formed a very close relationship with each and every one of them.

In her mother's eldest years, their weekly trips shopping and caring for one another became precious and priceless. Many of the events that happened in those later years were horrendous and terribly, terribly frightening, but with each event, came a family that only got closer.

As the years went by, Rebecca spent almost no time with her family. She loved her parents dearly and provided for them well but never forged a real relationship with them. She became the rich daughter who could be bragged about but secretly was said to not care enough to see her parents in their declining years.

After her brother, Sammy, was diagnosed with lupus; Reb and her family had come together to support him in whatever way they could, finally bringing him home where he would learn to live with his disease and be a part of the family he had left so many years before. With the exception of Billy, the family became close in a way that they had never been close when they were younger.

After her brother, Sammy, was diagnosed with lupus, Rebecca provided the best of everything for her brother, allowing him to stay in his own home in New Hampshire, never learning to live his life with the disease, never returning to his place of birth, and never having the close relationship with his parents, sisters, and brother-in-laws. Rebecca's brother was grateful for what his sister had done but wondered why she didn't care enough to visit him.

Reb had a love of cats and nature, gardening, traveling, and the ocean. Rebecca refused to allow any hobbies or pets that would distract her from her goals.

Reb had developed close, loving, and special relationships with her husband, parents, youngest brother, sister, grandparents, aunts, uncles, nieces, nephews, in-laws, friends, special friends at church, and most importantly, her son. Rebecca had no close relationship with any of these people, and Reb's son didn't exist.

Rebecca was wealthy. Reb was not. Reb was rich with the love of a family that loved her. Rebecca was not.

*　　*　　*

As Rebecca sat in her luxury living room on this evening three days before her fifty-first birthday, the difference between the two lives she had lived weighed heavily. On the one hand, she was wealthy, safe, and secure, at least materially. Her family was secure, at least materially. Her brother, Billy, had never been able to do the terrible things he had done in Reb's lifetime. He was dead and could never hurt anyone again. Rebecca had accomplished great things. She had accomplished what she set out to do.

On the other hand, there had been a cost to her accomplishments and the way she had driven herself. She had a family but did not know them. She had had no love in her life because she was afraid of being hurt. She had no real friends because she didn't trust, and even though she never lost her love of God or her ability to pray, somewhere she must have lost her faith because she believed that only her actions would result in the thing that she desired the most, safety. Most of all, her careful planning and hard work had resulted in the one thing that hurt her the most. Her son had never been born.

It was at that moment that Rebecca saw things clearly. Some would call it an epiphany. Some would call it a revelation. Rebecca only knew that in this, she was absolutely right.

*   *   *

Reb had been sexually molested by her oldest brother. She had been beaten. Her bones had been broken, fractured, and she had been irrevocably scarred. Rebecca had been able to prevent that from happening.

*   *   *

On this night, three days before her fifty-first birthday, Rebecca came to a very clear understanding. She may have been able to prevent and escape what had happened to Reb, but she was just as much a victim. She had the memories of Reb. Everything that she had done was in reaction to the same thing. While in her lifetime, Rebecca's brother was prevented from abusing others and died young, nonetheless, the very memory of what had happened in her first life colored everything she would ever do. Either way, the damage that her brother, Billy, had done was permanent and couldn't be changed. It was what it was, and in that sense, Billy had won. The only difference was in the way that Reb and Rebecca lived their lives, one as a result of trying to survive and the other as a result of trying to escape the pain and be safe.

Rebecca had changed the past and made a new present. Her present was safe and secure but not the life she really wanted, not the life that was true to her heart. Rebecca was safe. Reb never had been. Rebecca could go on and never worry about another thing as long as she lived, but she would have to go on never trusting or giving anyone the chance to get close. Most of all, Rebecca would have to go on without the one thing that she had ever done right, without reservation and without regret. She would have to go on without the one thing that was most important, her son.

Her son. This was the one thing that Rebecca had adamantly refused to even think about in the many years since she had woken up on that day in 1965 with a new life and a new purpose. Distancing herself from her parents, her brother and sister and her relatives wasn't all that difficult to do. After all, they would be well taken care of. Not marrying her husband would not hurt him as he would never know the difference and would hopefully live a happier life without her. But her son, her wonderful son, was something different, and his not being born was something that she had refused to even think about. She had long since learned to push away the visions and ignore the dreams.

On this night, three days before her fifty-first birthday, the memories of her son came back, not just in flashes like before but in a flood, a torrent of memories, his birth, his growth, and the years of his young adulthood. Rebecca couldn't prevent it. The love and pride that Reb had felt hit her like a title wave and twisted in her stomach like a knife. The love that Reb felt for her husband, her parents, her sister, her brother, and her home pierced her as well. While Rebecca had protected her family, Reb had loved her family in a way that money could never touch. Rebecca missed her family and realized, finally realized, that just maybe, Reb had done more things right than she knew. Without Reb, Alex had never been born, and more than anything in the world, Rebecca wanted her son.

*   *   *

With a heavy heart, Rebecca sat back and let the tears flow. "Lord, you gave me a miracle and let me live my life again knowing what I knew and being wise. You gave me health and strength and purpose, and you let me do the things I thought I needed to do to make things right. You made me wealthy and safe. You let me give my family the same. Thank you. Thank you for letting me feel safe and letting them be safe. You knew. You were the wise one, and you knew. I'm sorry that I didn't understand, and I didn't have enough faith to realize that you knew better than I did. I miss my family. I miss my husband. I miss my friends, and I miss my son. Please, please bring me back. Please let me have my first life back. Give me back the life I was meant to live."

With tears and with a feeling of tiredness that she hadn't felt in fifty years, Rebecca went to her beautiful luxury bedroom and lay down, crying herself to sleep.

*   *   *

REB

She woke up and slowly opened her eyes. Her left arm hurt. The bed felt strange yet familiar. She reached over to the right and felt fur. She opened her eyes up further and saw a beautiful gray Persian cat. It was one of her cats. Yes. It was one of her cats. She knew where she was. Carefully guarding her injured arm, she got out of bed, put on her robe, and opened up the bedroom door. She went out of the bedroom and down the stairs. She entered the pantry and laundry room, the kitchen and then out to her office, all of which she and her husband had worked so hard on remodeling. She looked out her office window at the lilac bushes in need of cleaning and pruning and beyond that to the antique camper and the giant oaks. She was back in her wonderful old 1931 house. She was back! She was home! Reb was back.

Reb walked into the wonderful old living room and checked to make sure the dog, her husband's wonderful puggle, was there. There he was, stretched out on one of the sofas snoring away. Reb knew that she was alone as her husband would have left for work hours before. Then, she called her parents to check on them. They were fine and asked if there was anything that they could do for her. Reb told them that she would be over in a while, just to visit. She then called her brother to check on him. He was busy packing for his move but would come up if she needed him. She then called her husband to check on when he would be coming home. She wanted to have a meal ready. Finally, Reb called her son who by that time lived many states away and was working hard forging a life of his own. He didn't answer, so she left a message on his voicemail to call.

After her last call, Reb took a shower, dressed, and did her arm exercises. The arm was improving, and she was getting much closer to being able to work again. After doing the exercises, Reb puttered around the house and began looking at all the pictures and photographs scattered throughout. She had pictures of her grandparents, now long gone. She had pictures of her and her husband, her parents, her aunts and uncles, her sister, her brother, Sammy, nieces, nephews, in-laws, the dog, and her cats, and she had pictures of her son.

Yes, Reb was back. Thank God.

*   *   *

Three days later, Reb celebrated her fifty-first birthday with joy and without regrets. It was a quiet birthday with just Reb, her husband, and her brother. Her husband cooked a favorite meal, and the three of them played cribbage. Her mother and father called to wish her a happy birthday and to tell her how much she meant to them and how much they loved her. It was the perfect day.

*   *   *

During the next few weeks, Reb had much time to ponder both the life she had lived and the second life she had lived through Rebecca. It was during this time that after a lifetime of pain, fear and trauma, she finally understood and began to heal. As Reb's arm began to knit back together and gain mobility and strength, she was able to gradually return to work, starting with only minimal hours and building slowly back to full-time. This gave her some hope, but it wasn't the answer to what she really needed.

Reb needed what Reb had always needed—to understand, to learn when to accept and when not to, to stop feeling guilty that she hadn't been smarter, to stop feeling that she was somehow to blame for what had happened to her, to stop feeling that somehow she was less than what she should be or what others expected her to be, and finally, to trust herself and allow herself to be exactly who she was.

Reb was more than grateful for the "do over" that God had given her. She knew that she, just like Rebecca, could never tell anyone what had happened to her, this time because it was too fantastic to be believed, but she could take this time to reflect, to ponder, to ruminate, to rant and rave if she so chose, to let out a lifetime of thoughts and feelings and opinions long buried. Through her "do over" and the life that she had really lived, the life that she chose to come back to, Reb finally found her voice. She stopped simply reacting and adapting. She allowed herself to really think, to finally be true in her thoughts and feelings, and to not be afraid that she was doing something wrong, somehow earning the bad things. She stopped trying to do everything right and allowed herself to be okay with failure.

Reb realized that the true tragedy, the true crime of what Billy had done to her wasn't just the fractured legs or the broken ribs, although the cost to her was beyond what most people could even begin to imagine. The true crime, and it was a crime, wasn't even the sexual abuse. In the end and after all was said and done, the true crime was instilling a fear in her, a fear of so many things that she was too young at the time to even name, much less understand. Most of all, Billy had taken away her voice before she ever had a chance to find it. Reb had never been given a chance to be herself, think for herself, believe in herself, or even learn who she really was.

Over the next few weeks, Reb would have time to do the one thing that she most needed to do: be honest with herself in whatever way she needed to be. She needed to open the floodgates and not keep anything out, let her thoughts and her feelings and her opinions go where they would. Some of it would be reflective. Some of it might even be profound. Some of it would be a release, some ranting, some raving; but whatever it would be, it would be honest and true to Reb even if others might not agree with her thinking, her opinion, or her feelings.

*   *   *

One of Reb's primary assignments in her first position as a new medical transcriptionist was in doing the transcriptions for a psychiatric hospital. Over time, not only did she become very proficient at completing these types of transcriptions, but she also learned a lot about the way in which this branch of the medical profession thought, and she found it to sometimes be very disturbing.

First of all, Reb was amazed at the things that were sometimes said about patients and put in their permanent medical record. Reb knew that most people were not aware of the fact that their medical record was permanent and that what was said by one provider would carry on to the next and most often believed without question. Although these records were by law confidential, they could and were used by insurance companies, government agencies, courts, etc., and were often taken as gospel by the people who read them.

Reb also learned that most medical providers were very stubborn, loyal to their own, and generally did not believe a lot of what their patients said or were highly suspicious and said so, at least in their reports. In truth, what she saw in the psychiatric community often wasn't any more or less narrow minded than what she had experienced with the medical community in the treatment of her brother's illness. In their attempt to be as objective as the physical medical community could be, the psychiatric community tried to fit each patient's life into neat and restricted little categories and narrow ranges of what it thought was normal. Patients were always labeled, and to the psychiatric community, this was what determined how they were viewed and treated.

Reb felt that many times the labeling was extreme. Reb had transcribed cases in which the patient did not drink alcohol, use illicit drugs, or smoke cigarettes, yet because the person drank a couple of cups a coffee a day, they were labeled as a caffeine abuser. When people said they had an occasional beer or alcoholic drink, they were labeled as an alcohol abuser or at least suspected of such. Smoking cigarettes was automatically labeled as nicotine dependence, which of course in most cases it was. Patients who had been placed on narcotics legitimately for pain control would eventually become addicted and after a certain amount of time were labeled as benzodiazepine abusers, opiate abusers, or some other type of drug abuser and then were treated the same as people who took the drugs to get high. If these same patients were the victim of a false and malicious report against them, both the medical and psychiatric community were quick to take their pain medication away, drop them from services, and not give a damn about how this affected the patient.

There was a lack of understanding and compassion for patients with medical conditions that caused chronic pain, and there was extreme paranoia in both the psychiatric and general medical community in prescribing pain medications that would help. People who had suffered catastrophic events such as a loss of loved ones, severe illnesses, loss of career, homelessness, or life-changing accidents were sometimes said to be overly "ruminative," "circumstantial," or obsessed with these themes. Patients who refused medication because they felt that the side effects from the medication were worse than the so-called cure were said to be "noncompliant" or "treatment nonadherent."

At the same time, Reb understood that there were people with true psychiatric illnesses such as with bipolar and schizophrenia and that the behavior of these people, when untreated, was often bizarre, delusional, sometimes obsessive and compulsive, and generally out of control, sometimes even violent.

Reb also understood that many, many patients had suffered from severe abuse or neglect during childhood and that this had somehow changed them in ways that people who hadn't suffered the abuse could never understand. After all, she was one of these people. She had just been determined not to let it affect her in the same way, and by some standards, she hadn't.

The rub was that for many of the stories Reb heard, she saw herself. Her heart often broke for the drug addicts, the children from broken homes, the children from abusive homes, and the children who ended up in foster placement, all of whom had the one thing in common that they had been mistreated by people they should have been able to trust. For whatever reason, these people simply were not able to escape the sadness, the fear, and the mistrust, and they traveled roads that would not only hurt themselves but hurt others.

For whatever reason, Reb had been able to escape these paths, and she was grateful. At the same time, she wanted to tell these people of abuse that at any point in time the choice was still theirs. The world of so-called normal people who had been fortunate enough to be brought up under the right circumstances, better circumstances, could never and would never really understand people like them and would always be their harshest critics. So be it. The drug addicts, the people who grew up in broken homes, the people who grew up in abusive homes and the people who grew up in foster homes could still reach deep down and somehow make decisions to change the direction of their lives. She had, if only on the surface, and she knew how difficult it was.

*   *   *

Reb also had transcribed many reports from doctors and other psychiatric providers who, by their very presentation, tone, and content, truly seemed to care about the patients and treated the people under their care with respect and compassion. It was the ones who didn't seem to care, the ones who rushed the reports, the ones who yawned and seemed bored when they spoke, the ones who seemed only to want to get the dictation done so that they could go home; these were the ones that concerned Reb. Maybe Reb was taking it too far, maybe too seriously, as was her nature, but she didn't think so. After all, these records, even if technically and legally confidential, were read and used by a lot of people whether for the benefit or the detriment of the patient.

*   *   *

Yes, Reb cringed when she heard some of the things that the psychiatric providers said about their patients, but the one thing, the very thing that bothered her the most, was the ridiculously narrow view that some people in the psychiatric community had toward Christianity, and for that matter, any subject that wasn't considered, by their standards, normal. It bothered Reb greatly that if a patient more than minimally mentioned that they believed in God or had faith, they might be labeled as having religious preoccupations or "delusions." If a patient was seen to pray or asked to pray for or with a provider, it would be described in their record as "religious preoccupation" or "religiosity." Reb understood that there were patients who truly were psychotic and as part of their psychosis took religion to a delusionary level, such as believing they were Jesus. However, there was a difference. In her opinion, much of the psychiatric community took their suspicion of religion too far and did not respect what was a very important part of so many lives, something that had been around for centuries more than the field of psychiatry.

Reb remembered one transcription in particular. It was a woman who was truly disturbed, had a recognized psychiatric disorder, and had been through some horrific circumstances. She had also long had a deep faith in God, had a long history of attending church and for many years lived a somewhat normal life with the support of her family and church. During her time in the hospital, she relied greatly on prayer to help her through. On one occasion, she asked the attending psychiatrist to let her pray with him and for him, and she asked to be allowed to pray in tongues. As expected, the psychiatrist rejected this request and insisted that it was part of her delusional condition. What he didn't understand was that this particular woman had a history of being part of the Pentecostal religion and in being so would see speaking in tongues as not only a normal expression of her faith but a much desired one. Reb understood this even if she had never shared in this type of religious expression. The psychiatrist, on the other hand, never considered this because he could only see things within his own very narrow point of view, the typical medical anti-Christian point of view, never wanting to believe in anything that couldn't be seen under a microscope or wasn't proven empirically, never considering that the science that he so revered just might have been created by God, the creator that he refused to believe existed. This type of rigidity was something that he and those like him often accused their patients of.

So in the end, the woman probably left the session with the idea that all the years of faith in God had somehow either been a delusion or just another symptom of how crazy she was, this from a doctor whose mission was to first do no harm.

* * *

There was another side of the coin. As disgusted as she was with the treatment that some people were given, Reb also found herself sickened by the way that many of these patients excused their own behavior because of the abuse they had experienced in childhood. This was a true enigma for Reb. She had transcribed some cases of childhood abuse that were worse than hers, but not many. Each time she listened to a story of sexual, emotional, and physical abuse, her heart broke for the victim, and she secretly wished revenge and justice for each and every one of them. She was one of them, and she understood better than anyone. At the same time, it didn't justify their own violence, sexual abuse toward others, abuse and neglect of their own children, horrible aggression toward others, laziness, drug addiction, and an unbelievable belief of entitlement that somehow other people owed them because of their past.

Reb understood that what had happened to them had been terrible and unfair and that they didn't deserve it. She understood the anger and resentment toward people who couldn't even begin to understand, the feeling that others didn't know how lucky they were, that they hadn't gone through what she did and others like her. She had also resented those who seemed to slide through life on a wave of good fortune, the lucky people who would never understand. So many times, she had felt hopeless and helpless and worthless just like the many patients' stories that she heard in her transcriptions.

The difference was that she had never and was never going to use it as an excuse to pass on the abuse. Her sister and youngest brother had never used it as an excuse either. Her oldest brother and the people like him who did such horrible things would have their day in judgment, but that was beyond what she could see now. Her life had been and was going to continue to be different. If she had succeeded in anything, she had never perpetuated the abuse she had lived through toward her own son, and she continued to believe that all people deserved to be treated with dignity and respect; all people except those like Billy.

*   *   *

Reb was grateful for the knowledge that her relatively new career in medical transcription had given her. It gave her an understanding that if the psychiatric community ever got a hold of her and heard her story, they would never believe it and would have a field day. She didn't know what label they would give her but could imagine that there would be a number of them. For that matter, her family's take on her story wouldn't be any different. She would go through yet again another round of not being believed, only this time she really could understand why.

Reb knew without a shred of doubt that what had happened to her, her "do over," really had happened and had been meant to be. It had not been a dream. She wasn't psychotic or delusional. It had been real, and she was meant to learn from it.

*   *   *

Reb really didn't know where to begin. There was so much to think about, so much to come to grips with. What should be first? Anger? Fear? Mistakes? Regret?

Reactivity? Hope? She had been through so many emotions, and she needed to face them all, the good and the bad.

*　　*　　*

Hope. Hope was the thing that Reb would begin with. In her early days, it was what gave her optimism and strength. Even after all the years of her brother's abuse, Reb was still an optimist. She still had hope. When young, Reb believed what her parents had taught her, that working hard and trying would mean that life would get better, safer, wealthier and that you would enjoy your accomplishments, the fruits of your efforts. It would take many, many more years for her to learn that this was a myth, at least for people like her, and in time, her hope dissolved. Reb knew that even after the revelation of having lived another life through Rebecca, it would take a miracle for the hope and optimism of her youth to return.

Reb had built her first career and her family on hope, despite the mistakes she had made and the misfortunes that happened over the years. She had been successful in her first career partly because of the determination that she had but mostly because of the hope that she had for her students, hope that her parents had given her but that everyone and everything else seemed determined to take away. When the injuries that her brother had given her resulted in her losing her career, Reb's ability to hope took a serious hit.

Even after this and during the very difficult time that followed the end of her first career, Reb continued to express hope to others, to her husband concerning their finances and saving all that they had worked so hard to achieve, to her brother concerning every part of his life, to her parents concerning their health and the stress of being elderly, to her sister concerning the needs of her niece, and to her son in whatever circumstances he found himself at the time. The only one that she couldn't express that hope to any longer was herself. She just didn't believe in it anymore. Hope was for other people, not her. Reb knew that God had answered many prayers over her life and given the many small miracles and a few big ones, and she was thankful, but returning her trust in the ability to hope for the things that she really needed was a major miracle, one that had been dashed too many times. For her, it was much easier to realize that hope was gone. It was at least a comfort that Reb could finally admit this and not hope anymore.

*   *   *

Reactivity. This was the next one to tackle. Many years ago, one of Reb's pastors had noted quite honestly that Reb was reactive whenever something happened that she strongly disagreed with. In actuality, he was both right and wrong. Reb had had a great deal of patience during her time as a teacher/therapist and rarely reacted with anger even in the most challenging of occasions, and she had many of those. Equally so, when Reb was teaching Sunday School and Junior Church or directing church holiday plays, she was also extraordinarily patient. The type of reactivity that her pastor had been talking about was a very negative, somewhat angry and definitely strong behavior that came through when Reb felt treated unjustly and when she felt her back was to the wall. It happened without thinking. It didn't happen often, but when it did, Reb was a tiger and backed down to no one.

It happened in church when a couple of new members of her church wanted to take her preschool and Junior Church rooms and turn them into one large room for the teenage program they were starting, thereby moving Reb and her kids upstairs into one very small room. It happened with certain things her husband said or did. It happened at certain very challenging times when raising her son. It happened in her first career when a particular special education teacher behaved outrageously and the school administrator did nothing to stop the behavior. It happened with certain parents who also behaved outrageously. It happened when her job required sixteen-hour days and then demanded more. It happened when her family did not believe her about the reality of what her oldest brother had done to her.

In all these circumstances, Reb was usually justified in reacting the way that she did and in expressing her distress, anger, and unwillingness to accept the things that happened. These were times when Reb was right and in retrospect knew it.

The other type of reactivity, the type that her pastor had been right about, even if he didn't understand why, was the type of reactivity that Reb felt internally, the type that people who had been abused like she was often expressed inwardly but never willingly showed. This reactivity was all about survival. It was about a need to watch closely, to listen closely, to be aware of danger, to react to danger, and to solve the problem. In psychiatric terms, it was called hypervigilance and had everything to do with fear and mistrust.

*   *   *

Reb had long been a little unusual for her gender or at least the more old-fashioned view of her gender. While she was a nurturer, she was more aptly a problem solver, the role that men liked to think of themselves as being the best at. In truth, Reb was a better problem solver than most men, something that she understood came from her background of surviving, not just abuse but very severe abuse. Reb's ability to react and problem solve was one of the things that had been most useful to the administrators and teachers that she worked with during her years as a speech therapist and special education coordinator. It had also made her a very good therapist because she could fairly quickly identify the problem and the steps that it would take to, if not cure the student's problem, at least improve their situation. She was so good at this that it became one of the things that burned her out as she became more and more in demand and was spread far too thin. Reb now understood that she really had had a very good mixture of nurturing, calmness, and problem-solving ability, but it was her reactivity that made her stubbornly strong when she needed it. It bothered her that this reactivity had come from such a negative source. After her forced early retirement, her reactivity had seemed to stop being useful and had reverted back to the hypervigilance and lack of trust that had been learned in childhood. Like her sense of hope, Reb wondered if she would ever again be able to regain a sense of control.

*   *   *

Regret and mistakes. Reb had a hard time separating the two. Reb had a lot of regrets, and she had made a lot of mistakes.

She was proud of some things. She had been the first one in her family, even her extended family, to earn a master's degree, something her grandmother would have been proud of. She was proud of the fact that she had earned this degree on her own, working to pay her own way through and support herself. She was proud of her son and the fact that even though she was a single mother in the early years, she had been able to be a good mother and the best provider that she could be. She was proud of the job that she had done during her long career as a speech therapist and a special education coordinator. She was proud of how many children she really had helped. She was proud of the time she had spent fully devoted to her church and the years that she had taught Sunday School, Junior Church, Vacation Bible School and directed the holiday plays. She was proud that at the age of forty-eight, she had been able to retire from one career out of necessity and learn a new and equally difficult career in just a few short months. These were the things that she knew she had done right. It was about time that she gave herself credit where credit was due.

Oh, but there were so many things that she had done wrong, so many mistakes, so many regrets.

Her first mistake had been thinking that not telling was the right thing to do. In her childhood, Reb didn't tell because she was under a constant threat that if she did, worse things would happen with the worst being that she would die. Reb's mistake was that she believed it, and her regret for this decision was lifelong. Yet Reb now understood that even if it had been a mistake and even if she did regret it, the decision was an understandable one, and she needed to forgive herself for it. She had been a very young child when the abuse started and a young child when the worst of the abuse had happened. She had had no one to talk to and no one to lead her in the right direction. Her reactivity had been one of an instinct to survive, and that had not been a mistake.

* * *

The mistakes that Reb had made in her late childhood and early teens were ones that she deeply regretted but ones that she now understood. Starting smoking at the age of twelve would become a livelong addiction that she would never shed. The drinking and marijuana use of her early teens, as well as hanging around a crowd that was anything but good for her was something else that she regretted yet at the same time understood. These people were the first people that she felt safe with, the first people she actually had fun with, even if in the wrong way. She was part of a group that did not beat her or sexually abuse her. She wasn't made fun of for her poverty because most of them were poor as well, and for the most part, she was accepted or at least treated better than she had ever known before. Reb also understood that as her behavior changed into something she didn't like, she had been wise and strong enough to leave before there was no return. The things that she had done then had also been understandable. She had done no harm to anyone but herself, and she needed to let go of the regret.

Most of her time in high school had been time well spent and something she did not regret. She had been a good student, had worked hard, and for the most part, had kept herself out of trouble. For a long time, Reb did regret her first serious relationship because in the end, she had not been true to herself and trusted this first love, given him something precious and had then been abandoned. The teenage Reb had modeled this first relationship after her parents and had been convinced that it would be lifelong. Of course, the older Reb knew that it really had just been a case of a first love gone wrong, that it hadn't been his fault or her fault, and that it was something that happened to most people. Her parents, after sixty-two years of marriage, were a rare case. The older Reb understood that her first love hadn't really been a mistake, just a rite of passage into adulthood, something that she no longer needed to regret.

The next thing for Reb to regret was her first marriage. If Reb was honest with herself, it was true that she had probably married on the rebound even if at the time she really had loved the man that she married. But she was just too young, and so was he. While it was something that in her early adult years she regretted and knew to be a mistake, in her older years, she realized that it was yet again another rite of passage and something that she needed to forgive herself for and put properly in its place, something else that she no longer needed to regret.

One of the greatest regrets in her life and one that would take her years to forgive herself for was the fact that she had been the first one in her family to have a baby out of wedlock. It was a very difficult and painful time for Reb, not because of the baby that was born, God, no. This baby, this wonderful child was the greatest miracle that Reb had ever known, and she did not regret his birth. The regret was in the way in which it had happened and the fact that she hadn't been able to protect her child from the circumstances of his own birth. She had tried. God, how she had tried.

*   *   *

Soon after the demise of her first marriage, Reb had met Alex's father and had fallen hard. Reb was still in a place in her life where her emotions and feelings tended to rule her, at least in her personal life, and she quickly fell for this man. For a while, the morality that she had been brought up with kept her from making the same mistake that she had made with her first boyfriend. However, her sense of morality did not last for long. By March of the next year, Reb was pregnant by a man who didn't know the meaning of monogamy, didn't want to know, and simply didn't want the responsibility. Reb found herself alone. When pregnant and during the few times that Alex's father was with her, Reb was scorned by his relatives, talked about, and treated like the slut that they wanted her to feel that she was. Her own family and friends didn't treat her much better. Her precious grandmother demanded that she not visit them. Neither her friends nor much of her family ever gave her a baby shower, and no one from his family or her family were there when her son was born. Her son's father would not make himself available to fill out and sign the papers that would declare him as the father.

It is no wonder that Reb felt so much shame. The older Reb understood that the shame and regret really should never have been hers. It should have been theirs. While her behavior had been a mistake, the birth of her son wasn't, and their treatment of her had been wrong. Her son really was a miracle, a miracle that Reb recognized from the day he was born. This young Reb had no idea of how much of a miracle he was. Thanks to her older brother and the things that he had done, Reb would never be able to have another child.

*   *   *

Thank God that the shame that was heaped on Reb and the shame that she felt never, at least she hoped, had ever tarnished her son. While Reb regretted some of the things that she had done and knew that she made mistakes over the years, she was a good mother, a loving mother, and a tiger of a mother when she needed to be. Her son hadn't been easy to raise, but he had been worth every moment of it. Throughout the years, Reb would make choices that were sometimes right, sometimes wrong, but always in what she thought to be in his best interest at the time. She hoped that God would forgive her for whatever mistakes she made yet protect and give her son the best life possible. In this, Reb was no different than most mothers, and she had no regrets.

*   *   *

During most of the next years, Reb did little that she could think of as regretful, at least not on her part. She knew that she had done the right things in working hard for her students and her family. Yes, she had made some mistakes, but they were minor errors in judgment and never anything that was different from what other people did. She had remarried, a good thing even if challenging at times, but certainly nothing to regret or to feel was a mistake. She had continued in a job for which she loved the children but hated everything else, again, not a mistake but admittedly a source of regret. She had continued in this job for a lot of reasons, the biggest being the security of her immediate family, namely her son. In the reality of things, this wasn't a mistake, just a reality that Reb had lived with and understood at the time for what it was, again, not any different from what other people had to do to survive.

Leaving the job was also nothing to feel regret for. It was not a mistake but a necessity. The injuries that her oldest brother had given her made it necessary for her to leave, and even if Reb had had a lot of anger and resentment about this, the truth was that if she had not been physically forced out of her first career, she would have eventually left anyway because she was burned out. The parts of her job that were relentlessly stressful and enveloped her twenty-four hours a day finally pushed her out the door, and she never looked back.

It was now almost four years since she had left, and she still had never had any regrets and had no desire to return. Leaving had not been a mistake but the right choice in every way. This was an important revelation for Reb. It was something that she couldn't completely hang on her childhood, a frightening yet normal change in life that was done for a variety of reasons, only partially because of the damage.

In the ensuing months and years, life would be difficult yet at the same time better than it was before. Reb had been able to shed the huge amount of stress that being a speech/language and special education specialist in the public schools had continually heaped on her over the years. She was no longer living with this job that never let her sleep without dreaming about it, this 24/7 job that was always so heavy on her shoulders and took so much from her personal and family life. She no longer spent night after night writing reports, evaluating tests, and making plans. For the first time in thirty years, she felt that her life was in her own hands, that she actually had a chance to live a life that was more on her own terms in a way that she had never known.

There were many times when this change made things very difficult for Reb and her husband, particularly financially, and there were times when they were really frightened by the unforeseen things that happened to them, no longer having the financial cushion that Reb's teaching salary had provided them. There were also many challenges with her family and with his, particularly hers. In some ways, it was more of an adjustment for Reb's husband as his work life should have remained the same but couldn't because of the limitations of what Reb could do. During these months and years, their marriage was put to the test. Somehow though, it survived and continued to survive. All this, even the tough times, were not things that Reb either regretted or felt in any way that she had made a mistake. Many times since her retirement from teaching she had been in a place of depression and even desperation, but somehow she and her husband made it through. Somehow, Reb continued to look for and find kernels of hope, at least until she injured her arm and couldn't work anymore.

At this point, the injury had taken all control away from her, and she could do nothing. At this point, she snapped and could see no way out. At this point, Reb was tired and really didn't care whether she lived or died. This was when her wish for a second chance, a "do over," began.

*   *   *

After returning from her "do over" and the life that Rebecca had lived, Reb realized that the changes and the challenges that had happened to her since retiring had as much to do with her as it did with the way in which Billy had broken her body. Reb could and would never rule out the damage that Billy had done and how this had affected what her body would allow her to do. She also could and would never be able to rule out how Billy's abuse had affected her mind. At the same time, somehow, she was still in control of her own thoughts and decisions, and it was up to her to live the rest of her life in a way that was true to Reb, with mistakes but without the regrets that her childhood had given her. Reb couldn't do anything about what her brother had done to her. Reb couldn't do anything about the damage it had done. Reb couldn't do anything about the damage it was still doing. At the same time, Reb needed to learn a very important lesson. It was time for Reb to like herself, to be okay with who she was, to change the things that she could, to stop beating herself up for the things she couldn't, and to simply live the life that God had meant her to live, whatever that was. When all was said and done, Reb didn't have the answers. She had wanted them but never found them. At this point in her life, Reb just needed to live. It was wonderful that in this time of reflection and honesty, she could finally see this.

*   *   *

Still though, Reb had at least a couple more things to think about and work through, fear and anger.

Oh boy. These were the two worst, the ones that had most plagued Reb, one very silently and one very much on the surface.

Fear. Reb had worn this one in and on every fiber of her being ever since the first time her oldest brother had beaten her. It was the one emotion that colored everything she did in her childhood and much of what she did for all of her adulthood. The fear was there because a child of abuse is constantly afraid that everything they do will result in something worse, something bad, or something that will be taken away. For Reb, her fear was first engrained by Billy's threats and by the actions that he took against her. After all, aside from killing her, he had done the things that he said he would do. He had done much more, things that she didn't even understand at the time. Any good things that happened or were modeled for Reb became something to fear that would be taken away or just wouldn't work out.

Reb's early relationships were modeled after her parents, and she expected that the good things, the things you earned would always last and remain the same, just as her parents' marriage had lasted. In Reb's teenage and early adult years, she would be utterly destroyed when relationships that she had didn't work out. After all, she must have done something terribly wrong for these people to leave her because truly good things for good people were meant to last. When her first relationship ended, then her first marriage, and then the relationship that produced her son ended, Reb was convinced that she just didn't deserve to be loved. After all, she must be a very bad person to have had a brother do the things that he did and then so many others hurt her as well. After this and as time went on, she left relationships, whether they were just friendships or something more because she feared that they would end anyway or because she would be somehow betrayed or maybe just because she simply deserved the punishment. In any case, by the time Reb was in her twenties, she had learned that she wasn't worthy and that people would always hurt her, always. As she got older, Reb feared more and more things. She trusted less and less and feared the loss of security and safety the most. It was a miracle that her second marriage lasted.

The older Reb understood that she had long been most afraid of losing security and safety. It was the one thing that she had never had as a child and had earned in very difficult steps as an adult. It was one of the things that had made leaving her first career such a courageous act. The search for safety was the one thing that children of abuse, any abuse, needed the most.

In her "do over," Rebecca had been able to insulate herself in a world of wealth to a point where she was never in danger and always safe. Rebecca had found a way to be both safe and secure, one of the things that Reb most wanted and something that Reb knew that the uncertainty of would plague her for the rest of her life. It was one of the lifelong weaknesses that truly did come from the severe abuse she had lived through. In the end, for the fifty-one-year-old Reb, it wasn't going to be something that could be solved. This now innate fear was something that Reb would never be able to shed but something that she could at least acknowledge was always there and understand why. The best she could do was to understand that when this automatic reaction happened, this terrible knot in her stomach, the anxiety and panic attacks, and all the other symptoms that happened, which was often, she could recognize it, step back, think it through, and ultimately control it, at least most of the time. It was a comfort for Reb to finally understand this even if she couldn't make it go away.

*   *   *

Anger. This was an easy one for Reb, and she had a lot of it, most of it under the surface and never shown to others. Her gentle nature and deep love for her family had never allowed her to really express it, but anger she had and she had had a lifetime of reasons for it. Rebecca had prevented all the circumstances that had made Reb angry. Reb had lived through every one of them.

Where to start? The obvious place. First and foremost was her oldest brother, Billy. He had sexually molested her on three different occasions. He had beaten her and thrown her down flights of stairs, not just once, but more times than Reb could count. He had broken her ribs, fractured her legs and her pelvis. He had bullied, threatened, and terrorized her in so many ways, much that she had repressed and much that kept coming back to her in nightmares. He had beaten and molested her beloved brother, Sammy, in ways that Sammy still could not talk about. He had bullied, threatened, and beaten her sister and threatened her mother. He had bullied and beaten up half of the neighborhood. In adulthood, he had bullied and abused the first two of his children. In adulthood, he had abused at least two of his wives. In adulthood, he had found a way to make himself wealthy by yet more deceit.

At the time of Reb's fifty-first birthday, her brother, Billy, had lots of money, didn't work, and was living high, doing exactly what he wanted to do, living in a large expensive house, traveling the world, and living his dream with no remorse and never owning up to the things he had done. Somehow, he had gotten away with it all and had never been held accountable.

Yes. Reb was angry. Reb was pissed. She had a right to be.

The older, wiser Reb had long since made a huge effort to stop giving Billy the right to make her angry. Being angry at Billy only took energy that she didn't have to waste. Not allowing herself to give into the anger was the one thing that she could control.

But the truth was that Reb couldn't really end the anger because she had never come to terms with it. The truth was that Reb could not but had to accept what had happened to herself and to the others in her life that she loved. After all, she couldn't change it. Rebecca's life had changed the acts, and it was the best thing that Rebecca did in her second chance. In Reb's world, however, what was done was done, and she had to learn to live with it. Reb could learn to live with what had happened, and for the most part, she really had, at least most of the time. She now understood that there would always be times when the memories would come back in flashbacks or nightmares and that this would probably happen for the rest of her life. She could and would go for long periods of time without this happening and then would suddenly begin going through it all over again. This too, if she had to, she could accept.

What she still had a hard time with, what still made her angry was the fact that her brother, Billy, had gotten away with it all, had no remorse, no admission of the things that he had done, and in fact, continued to flourish financially and materially, mostly through lying, cheating, and ill-gotten gain.

*   *   *

Reb felt some comfort in that her husband, her sister, and her brother, Sammy, felt the same way and often expressed their anger as well. They too had been victims, Sammy and Sissy, victims of the abuse and Reb's husband, a witness of the fall-out from what his wife, sister-in-law, and brother-in-law had experienced.

At the end of her "do over," Rebecca had figured out that even though in Reb's lifetime, Billy had not been held accountable for his actions, he had lost most of his family, even if it didn't matter to him.

After living the "do over," Reb understood that family was the most important thing and that no amount of success and money could or would earn this or give it to you. Billy might not appreciate or value family, but he had lost most of his family just the same. In the end, Reb, her brother, her sister, and her husband would probably always be angry at the unfairness of what Billy had done and gotten away with. In the end, at least for Reb, she had to make due with the thought that Billy's final judgment hadn't happened yet.

*   *   *

The anger from the events of Reb's childhood was obvious and absolutely understandable. The anger from that point onward was much less obvious and kept even better hidden than her anger from the abuse.

*   *   *

Reb came from an extended family that was very religious, strict Baptists that taught forgiveness, kindness, and always putting the other person first. Even if Reb didn't learn this from the church during her childhood, it had been gently encouraged by her parents, and it was an inborn part of Reb's nature. This trait, or at least the knowledge of what she should do and how she should feel, became even further entrenched once Reb joined the Baptist church in her early thirties. Yet Reb was just as human as anyone else, despite what the Baptist church taught you that you should be, and she felt anger about certain things that she had never really dealt with. The fifty-one-year-old Reb was ready and willing to admit to the many things and people that she was angry with. It was one more thing that needed to be dealt with rather than buried.

*   *   *

Even when still very poor and in college, Reb had put others first and helped her friends in any way she could. Many of her friends, her closest friends, were working people who didn't have cars or other material things. Reb had an old car and used it to take friends places even when it cost her money and time that she didn't have. When these friends got married, she went to their bridal showers with the best gift she could afford. When these friends had babies, she helped to plan and went to their baby showers with more than what she could afford. When problems happened, she was there if she could be. She even lent her second wedding dress to a good friend who never returned it.

When Reb became pregnant out of wedlock, most of her friends were not there for her. These same people who had been a part of her life for many years did nothing to help her or support her. They did not give her a baby shower. When she asked her best friend to be her partner in Lamaze because the baby's father would have nothing to do with it, the friend would only do it if she could be the first one to hold the baby, not the baby's father. On Reb's twenty-third birthday, Reb was invited to a tenth anniversary party for a friend and her husband. She was six months pregnant, scared, and alone. Reb brought a nice gift. No one, not even her best friend, wished her a happy birthday. Reb was very hurt by all these events.

At the time, she thought that she really must be a terrible person to deserve this treatment. In time, she would become quite angry about it but say nothing. Eventually, she would simply drop out of their lives and never see them again. At fifty-one, she was still angry and realized that she really hadn't deserved this treatment and had done nothing to deserve it. She had been a friend. They hadn't. They had been wrong. Understanding that someone or some people could have been wrong was comfort enough. These people had been shallow and uncaring, and she was glad that she had left these people behind.

When Reb became pregnant out of wedlock, her very religious extended family were naturally ashamed of her and did not want her presence in their homes, particularly her grandmother who was quite vocal in saying she didn't want outsiders to ask questions. They did give her a baby shower consisting in attendance of her mother, her grandmother, one of her aunts, and one cousin. It was a solemn occasion where no one would look below her neck and rarely looked her in the eye.

Reb received the same treatment from the baby's father's family only without the baby shower and with statements by that family's members of what a slut she must be.

When Reb gave birth to her son, there were no members of either family there, none, just the baby's father and the one friend who was to be her Lamaze partner but because of Reb's C-section wasn't needed.

Throughout the months of her pregnancy and following the birth of her son, Reb was deeply hurt by the actions of all these people, yet after all, again, she must be a truly horrible person to deserve such treatment. The fifty-one-year-old Reb knew that she had a right to be angry and that she had hadn't deserved this.

*   *   *

When Reb became pregnant out of wedlock, her boyfriend at the time questioned whether the baby was his. Reb had never been what in today's terms would be considered loose. Of course, the baby was his. When Reb became pregnant, the baby's father was quite vocal in saying that he wasn't ready for the responsibility and that the responsibility was hers. He wanted to be footloose and fancy-free and said so. When the baby was born, the baby's father was quite vocal in saying that he couldn't handle or afford the responsibility and that she was on her own. This was another one that Reb didn't deserve, but her son was precious and deserved everything that she could give to him.

Her son would become the best thing that ever happened to her and the one thing that for which all the hurt and betrayal would be worthwhile, yet the anger that Reb felt toward her son's father would last a very long time.

The fifty-one-year-old Reb was no longer angry, maybe disgusted with what her son's biological father had done, but not angry. This was one of those things that Reb believed would be handled by a higher power when her son's biological father met his maker, yet still she could finally say that she had had a right to be angry and didn't deserve the way she had been treated.

In the ensuing years, Reb would express her anger at her son's biological father and would continue to battle his irresponsibility. In the end, however, her son grew up to be the intelligent, strong, and wonderful human being that she knew he would be despite his origins, despite his biological father's irresponsibility, and despite the scarlet letter that had been placed on his mother by so many. The end result for her son and what he would become was all that Reb had ever hoped for or wanted and for this, all was forgiven.

*   *   *

Reb had a lot of anger toward her first career.

During twenty of Reb's twenty-four-year career as a therapist/teacher/ sub-administrator, Reb was often frustrated, but she almost always kept it to herself. For twenty-three out of her twenty-four years, Reb worked in the same school. She had a reputation as a very kind and patient person who could be relied on. In truth, she really was the kind and patient person that everyone expected her to be. However, she also worked closely with a bully, a lady named Francine, whose power and control over the school continued to gain in strength, mostly because her bullying was more than aggressive, and people tended to do what she wanted them to just to get her off their backs. She was an intimidating and controlling person who delved in every aspect of the school process including being active in politics. She once told Reb that she worshiped her own need to control as much as Reb worshiped God. The woman was truly jaded and was rarely held back, partly because the administration in the school was weak and like everyone else would do whatever necessary to appease her so that she would simply go away.

Reb was often a particular target of Francine, especially when Reb did something that earned her any accolades or a power that wasn't Francine's. Over the years, Reb was one of the only people who would face off with her, document the abuse and ridiculous actions of this person, and demand that action be taken. In each instance, Reb would launch the necessary lengthy documentation, keep records, and in one instance, refuse to communicate with Francine except through writing where she could keep records of everything that happened. At the same time, Reb had time after time worked closely with Francine and stood by her when she thought it was the right thing to do. Francine was an excellent teacher on her good days, which was in fact hundreds of times, and when not in bullying mode, she was a powerful advocate for her students, something that Reb both shared and admired. Yet despite Reb's support and her rightful complaints, over the years, Francine was somehow able to continue on and tear people down, and like most bullies, her behavior only got worse. Most of the other teachers in the building came to Reb with their anger, complaints, and total exasperation in how to deal with this person, this special education teacher who had so much power over the welfare of their own students.

In time, Reb too became burned out over dealing with Francine and at the time of Reb's early retirement could certainly say that one of the major reasons she left was because of this bully.

The message? Bullies don't just happen to young people, and bullying in any form and in any place is abuse—period. The anger? Francine, to the best of Reb's knowledge, was still working at the same school, and most of the teachers that

Reb had worked with had found a way to leave the building. Francine was yet another one that got away with it and continued to flourish, this in a place that was supposed to be safe for all.

Reb's anger at the things that had happened during her first career, however, was not all centered on Francine's bullying. She was angry and disgusted that Francine had never been stopped, and she feared for the welfare of the staff and the students. However, this bully was allowed to continue to do what she did simply because of a weak administration that would neither recognize nor act upon what was right in front of them, something that seemed to happen in every facet of society. If something irrevocable did happen, it was the fault of the administration, and they would have to live with the consequences. In the twenty years of working with Francine, Reb had done everything possible to correct or at least improve the situation. She had no regrets, and the blame was truly theirs.

*   *   *

Reb's personal anger had just as much to do with the way that she was treated at the end of her first career. Over the years, Reb had participated in, helped plan, and been a gift giver for many of her coworkers. Some of these events were for long-term employees who were retiring, and the events were always nicely done. Many of these events were baby showers, wedding showers, and milestone birthdays, often for people who hadn't been working for the school for very long. These events were always well put together as well, some more lavish or thoughtful than others depending on the popularity of the guest of honor or the particular clique the planner or planners happened to belong to. These events always took place either before or after school and sometimes even on a weekend evening. Over the years, Reb spent a small fortune on gifts for each of these people, never lavish but always well thought out. For teachers and specialists, the school would often have a surprise assembly for the retiring person so that the students and/or parents could express their appreciation.

After twenty-three years of faithful service to this one school, Reb's speech therapy assistant planned a small luncheon during the school lunch hour complete with grilled hot dogs, a couple of salads, and a hand printed sign in black ink with her name misspelled. None of the long-time staff members, the people Reb had worked so hard for for so many years had anything to do with the planning. Many of the staff did not attend or stopped in quickly. Francine, whom she had had to work with closer than anyone else and had often rescued other teachers from, did not attend. The principal never told the students that she was retiring, and not even a card signed by her students was given. Reb was deeply, deeply hurt.

By the last day of her contract, Reb was so hurt that she could not make herself stay through the day with the students gone, the last staff assembly occurring and the staff getting together for an end-of-the-year barbeque. On her last day, she went in early, finished cleaning out her office, placed her laptop on the principal's desk, and left the building. When she left the building, she swore that she would never step inside it again and would never willingly see these people who had been so cold and callous, and she never did.

When Reb thought about it now, she knew that a part of her would always be hurt and angry over the cold and unfeeling way she had been treated. Anyone who had dedicated themselves the way she had would be hurt. The new revelation was that she understood that this anger and hurt and the anger and hurt that she carried from the time of her pregnancy and the early years of her son's life were things that were not a product of her childhood. These were normal and happened in one form or another to everyone.

It was good to be honest with herself and admit that she was still angry, still hurt. It was good that she could allow herself to admit that she still felt hurt and angry and not feel the need to bury the feelings and pretend they weren't there. It was good that she could realize that these were bad things that sometimes happened to good people and that these things were part of life. It was good that she could realize that even with these painful events, she had had many more good things that had happened to her and continued to happen to her and many more caring people in her life who had treated her like she mattered. In the end, Reb truly felt that the people who had been so cold and callous were not worth her tears. It was good that Reb could finally say that these people had been cold and callous, and she had been worthy of something better.

In the end, it was the distinction between all the fallout from the abuse, the emotional, and the physical results to her, to Sissy, and to Sammy, the many things that Reb could lay directly on her oldest brother's actions; this versus the things that unfortunately happen to everyone; this was what she most needed to be open and honest with herself about. This was the part that her "do over" had helped her to separate, and this was what she had learned that people like her needed to understand. No one's life, not hers, not her sister's, not her youngest brother's, not the many, many people whom Reb knew had suffered from abuse; none of them could ever really blame it all on the abuse. It was a reason but not an excuse, and surviving it was a choice. Reb's choice was to acknowledge the abuse, understand it for what it was, and let it make her stronger.

*   *   *

There was one word that had not been part of Reb's original list to contemplate. Forgiveness. This was the toughest one of all. This was the word that in church she was taught was a must and not a choice because of what Jesus had done for her on the cross. Because of this teaching, Reb often felt guilty when she knew she did not and could not follow this command. Reb was good at forgiving the little things and when she forgave people for those it was true to her heart. But Reb wasn't a liar, and the truth was that she didn't forgive some of the big ones. She didn't forgive her brother, Billy. She didn't forgive her so-called friends who hadn't been there when she so desperately needed them. She didn't forgive her son's biological father who had made a difficult situation even more difficult. She didn't forgive his family or her family for the way they had viewed her when she was anything but. She didn't forgive her former coworkers whom she had worked for so diligently. Most of all, she didn't forgive herself.

In one sense, Reb was glad that she could be honest with herself and admit these feelings instead of burying them as she would have in the past. At the same time,

Reb knew that this type of anger festered and would continue to fester if she didn't do something about it. In the end, she couldn't do anything to change the events or the people who had done these things. After all, the reality was that these people, for the most part, never realized the damage that they had done. Jesus had said, "Forgive them for they know not what they do." Just maybe there was something in that. With the exception of Billy, who knew what he did, Reb needed to give this one more time.

*   *   *

Finally, Reb thought a lot about what Rebecca had learned during the "do over" and what through Rebecca she had also learned. It was a lot. After all, through Rebecca, Reb had lived a second lifetime, very different from the one she had lived, safer, more successful, so many things that she could have been and done but didn't. Rebecca had gotten the jump on Billy and prevented what was to be. Rebecca knew the things that Reb would do that would harm her, keep her from reaching her potential, and avoided them. Rebecca forced herself to have the confidence that Reb never had. Rebecca forced herself to think and feel that she was worthy of good things and equal to others, and in time, she believed it. Reb was convinced that she was anything but worthy and had somehow done something to deserve the treatment that she got. Rebecca's new choices made her stronger and wiser in the ways that made her successful. The abuse that Reb had lived through and some of the choices she had made had ultimately made her weak. Rebecca's choices had made her strong.

At the same time, Reb's gentle and loving nature kept her loyal and close to her family, her students, her church, and her home. Rebecca's need to succeed supported her family but left them without her presence in their lives. Rebecca was alone and lonely. Reb was not.

In the end, it came down to a choice of what was most important, and God had allowed both Rebecca and Reb to make the choice. Rebecca and Reb were the same person, living two different lives, both with gentle and loving natures, sometimes wise and sometimes not, but both with a deep love for the people who were truly important in their lives. Rebecca had prevented the events, but she couldn't prevent the memories and realized that her answer to the abuse had really been no better than anything Reb had done. In fact, Reb's life had been the richer one: mistakes, warts, and all. Rebecca had made the right decision when she asked to come back.

*   *   *

In the end after all was said and done, Reb could only continue to try to be honest with herself. Yes, the abuse she had lived through had been terrible and the repercussions more than what anyone should ever have to experience. In truth, she would always believe that her oldest brother should and would be destined for hell no matter how he was able to avoid it on earth, but this again, was out of her hands and up to God. If God did decide to allow Billy into heaven, Reb had enough faith to understand that God would have his reasons. If not, well, God would also have his reasons for that. Her brother's judgment was out of her hands.

Reb could only continue to try to be honest with herself, to not think that she was somehow deserving of the worst, and to continue to work for and hope for better, if not the best. Reb would continue to be angry about certain things and to be honest about it and just maybe someday be able to let the anger go, but she was no longer going to bury what she thought or how she felt. She was going to continue to appreciate and love her family as fiercely as she ever had and wasn't going to give up on her dreams, even at the age of fifty-one.

*　　*　　*

For many of her adult years, Thanksgiving had been Reb's favorite holiday. While Reb loved Christmas and had wonderful memories of childhood Christmases and the Christmases when Alex had been young, it was Thanksgiving that over the years would become the most important to her. After she and her husband bought their house and as her parents aged and could no longer manage large family celebrations, Reb and her husband made a tradition of having Thanksgiving dinner at their house. It was a huge production and one that Reb looked forward to every year. There were years when they would have twenty or more for dinner with people staying over for several days afterward. Their home became known as holiday central. This year would be no different, and Reb was excited just as she always was.

Reb was back at work, working her evening shift as a medical transcriptionist and gradually working up to a full-time work week. Her arm was sore and slow to strengthen, but she was getting there. Normally, she would have the week of

Thanksgiving off, but this year, she would have to work because she had used all her vacation time following her injury. She would only have Thanksgiving Day off. Luckily, her husband, brother, sister, in-laws, and even her elderly parents were troopers and came to the rescue and did all the work except for her stuffing, which, like her grandmother's chocolate cake, was a recipe all her own.

When Thanksgiving arrived, Reb had everything ready: the two turkeys, all the fixings, the appetizers, and a beautifully set table complete with name cards for seating. She had sixteen people there: Her parents, her mother-in-law, her sister and her husband, her niece, her brother, her husband's nieces, her husband's sister, her husband's two brothers and their wives, her brother-in-law's mother-in-law, and finally, Reb's husband, Derrick.

*   *   *

Yes. Reb's husband, Derrick, her first and her second, one and the same. Their first marriage hadn't lasted. They were too young and needed time to grow up. It would be fate that they would meet again a few years later when Reb's son was two. What had brought them together in the first place was still there, and they would marry again in April of 1987, this time for keeps. Through the years, they would continue to grow and change, be challenged by life, love, fight, and make up again, both of them raising Alex into the fine young man he would turn out to be.

*   *   *

With the food served, they all sat in their places at the long, uneven series of tables in Reb and Derrick's very old living room in the old farmhouse at the top of a hill someplace in Maine.

To her left at one end of the table sat her father, her now eighty-one-year-old father, slowed, a little stooped, hard of hearing, a little slow in thought and memory, yet still having that same sparkle in his eye when he looked at his wife of now more than sixty-two years. Across from Reb sat her mother, her beautiful eighty-year-old mother, now able to walk only with a walker, with gray hair and a very stooped posture, but still as beautiful to Reb as she had always been. Her mother had changed a great deal over the years. As ill and feeble as she was in body, she was now a person of strong spirit and conviction, someone who Reb now respected and trusted more than anyone else in the world.

At the other end of the table sat her husband, her wonderful husband of nearly twenty-five years, the man whom she had loved and still loved and the man who had been through the worst and best of times with her.

In between the two ends of the table sat the other people who meant so much. Across from her was Sissy, her smart, strong, creative, and sensitive sister who never let anything, no matter how challenging, defeat her. Next to Sissy was her brother-in-law, a wonderful and brilliant man who had faced his own physical challenges and learned to live with them without rancor or bitterness. Beside him was her niece, her wonderful, vivacious niece who was the only female grandchild in the family, brave, unique, and talented in ways that she hadn't even discovered yet.

Beside Reb was her brother, Sammy, her wonderful, special brother who had overcome so much and learned to live with even more. She and Sammy shared a common bond that would forever make them the best of friends, extreme abuse and times of tribulation that made them both understand and respect each other in ways that they would never let each other down.

Then there was her husband's oldest brother and best friend, someone who could always be trusted. Beside him was his wife, Betty, one of Reb's most trusted and closest friends, both people who were very precious to Reb and her husband.

Across from them was her husband's youngest brother and wife, two people who had been through their own sort of hell yet had good hearts, were hardworking, and somehow managed to overcome what was one of the worst years for them. Beside Reb's youngest sister-in-law was her sister-in-law's mother, a dear lady who had been through the worst of all of them. She had lost her husband the spring before.

Finally, next to her husband was her mother-in-law, a very dear lady who somehow remained young in her heart no matter how old she was and who was very happy to be there with her children on this special day.

Like no other year, 2011 had been the worst for this family. Without exception, every single person sitting at that table had been through some of the most difficult times in their lives. Illnesses, extreme stress, injuries, poverty, and even death had affected them all. Yet somehow, on this day, God had brought them all together. Reb was wiser now, and she understood that this was a day and time to truly be appreciated. This was the reason why she had been given the gift of the "do over."

*   *   *

But wait a minute. Next to her brother's chair was an empty one with a place setting and no name card. Reb was sure that she had counted right and couldn't understand. Then something happened. She didn't know if it was instinct or hope, but for whatever reason, she turned around, and there he was. Standing tall and strong with a great big smile was Alex, her son, her wonderful, handsome twenty-seven-year-old son. Looking around, there was a mixture of tears, smiles, and laughter with her husband showing all three. "Hi, Mom. Happy Thanksgiving."

*   *   *

Even though the others didn't know this and wouldn't know why, Reb knew that this was her gift and a gift for her. For the third time in her journey in this person who wasn't given to tears, her tears spilled over, and she could do nothing to stop them. She hugged her son as if she hadn't seen him in a very long time. In truth, it had been more than fifty years. Reb hugged him and hugged him and hugged him, much to his embarrassment. Once calmed and with everyone seated, Reb began her yearly Thanksgiving prayer.

In years past, Reb had either rushed her Thanksgiving prayer or had asked someone else to say it because she was uncomfortable and simply couldn't say what was truly in her heart. This year, however, her prayer would be different, absolutely honest and without regard for form or time.

* * *

"Dear Father in heaven: This is your day, your day for your people to gather and say thank you for the many blessings you have given us throughout the year. This family has been through so much, so much more than what good people should ever have to go through. But we made it through and are together now. I pray that what each of us has endured has made us stronger. I thank you that this family has found strength in working together and helping each other. Maybe, that's the point and that's the blessing. Still, I ask you to make this next year better. Father, thank you for each and every person sitting at this table. I pray that next year will give us all the strength to face what we do not know, endure what is to be, and be together again next year at this time."

At this point, eyes were wet, and Reb ended the prayer with one last statement.

"And oh, by the way, Lord, thank you for bringing me back."

As everyone around her looked bewildered, Reb thought, "Maybe Billy didn't win after all."

*   *   *

There is a song, a special song, one of Reb's favorites, "Bridge over Troubled Water" by Simon and Garfunkel. Now, instead of hearing Cher's "If I Could Turn Back Time" in her head, Reb heard the beautiful words of Bridge. She didn't know the reason or the writer's inspiration behind the words of the song, but for her, the song held more meaning than anyone would ever know. For Reb, God had been and was her bridge, and so was her family, save one. Maybe she would never "shine" as in the words of the song, but through God's gift to her of the "do over," he had brought her to a place of honesty with herself, acceptance of the good and the bad, and appreciation for where her life journey had taken her, back to the people who loved her. It was something that most children of abuse never achieved, and for Reb, it was enough.

THE END

Well,

ALMOST . . .

ARTHUR

ARTHUR

There is a place far above the earth, somewhere straight above or to the left or the right, somewhere in the heavens in a realm unseen by the eyes of mortal man, a place that cannot be reached by rocket or shuttle or satellite. It is a place of incredible beauty, perfect peace, and understanding. It is a place for the children of faith after a time of trial, tribulation, and blessings on earth. It is a place filled with brilliant beings created by the one who created the heavens and the earth. It is heaven.

In this place are many angels, each with a purpose and a job created by the Father, some big, some small. In the entire scheme of things, Arthur's job was a small one but an important one.

The Father was the inventor and the master of miracles. Miracles came in all forms, some large, some small. Sometimes, mankind recognized the miracle. More often, they didn't. Once in a while, the miracles were obvious and couldn't be ignored. Sometimes, they were obvious yet were still explained away by his children. Many times, the miracles were small and happened in the midst of tragedy and misfortune. Most times, the unexpected was explained away by the children who did not choose to believe in Him. There were many who didn't, but He loved them anyway.

Then there was the unusual miracle, the gift of the "do over." Arthur was in charge of this one.

Arthur's office, if you could call it that, was state of the art, a millennium beyond the technology of man with tools incomprehensible to mankind, as was the place that he worked from. From here, he could see, hear, feel, and touch anything and anyone with nothing more than a thought. His boss was the all-knowing one, and everything came from Him. It was here that Arthur lovingly and faithfully did his job. He was the angel of the "do over."

Arthur had been doing this for many, many centuries, and he was a master at it but not, he knew, the master of it. The candidates for the "do over" were chosen by the boss, and it was Arthur's job to make them happen. There were always many candidates, all for different reasons and all from different places, cultures, and circumstances, but only one was chosen at a time. Yet time in heaven was a relative thing, and so there were many "do overs." Each was chosen carefully, each with a different ending that was already known by the boss, some expected, some magnificent, some simple, some profound, but always with progress and a blessing given.

Reb had been chosen for many reasons: first and foremost because she had a kind heart and soul; second because life had so deeply wounded her; and finally because she was so close to giving up without ever realizing what she really had. Being a woman of faith was not one of the boss's criteria. Faith never was. For some, the "do over" was given to lead to faith. Reb had already been blessed with hers.

No, Reb was chosen because she had heart and soul and courage. She just didn't know it.

In the end, Reb's "do over" did not give her wealth or fame or safety, the things she had thought would protect her. Reb's "do over" gave her an insight and understanding that she had never had and an appreciation for the things that really counted. As time went on, Reb would go through many more trials, tribulations, and triumphs, yet she would eventually gain a measure of safety and stability in her life. In time, she would also find peace.

So Reb's "do over" had been a success for the boss, as He knew that it would be.

Arthur already had his next assignment.

THE END

SOME FINAL THOUGHTS FROM THE AUTHOR

The writing of *Do Over* and the road to publication has been a bit of a roller-coaster ride complete with unexpected twists and turns and many challenges. *Do Over* did not begin with a plan or expectation of becoming a story, much less a book. It truly began as a journal and chronology of events from the writer's own lifetime, a way to express events and feelings that had long been buried and a way to deal with a true crossroads in life.

As the story began to unfold, the character of Reb was created and was used to tell a story that is partly true and partly fictional. With the first complete manuscript, I took a chance and sent it to a publisher. It was accepted as it would be with each publisher that would agree to consider it. In time, I let the people I trust, both family and friends, know what I had done, what I truly had felt inspired to do. The road toward publication was paved with many challenges including skepticism, most notably my own. With the skepticism came, the one thing that I hadn't really thought about, Reb's story hit a nerve, and I was stunned.

For the very few people who read *Do Over* before its publication, the story led to stories of their own, some stories from people close to me of events in their early life that I did not know about, painful stories of abuse that had long been buried but that they felt safe and somehow comforted to be able to talk about. In some ways, Reb's journey and her healing opened a road for them as well. One of the people most affected was "Sissy," my real sister, and she asked that I end this writing with my own thoughts. So for you Sis and for anyone and everyone who has ever been a victim of abuse, any kind of abuse, here goes. This is what I really think, and it is expressed from a person who has lived through it and with the memories of it for more than fifty years.

*   *   *

Abuse is not simply a matter of the abuser and the abused. There is always a bigger story and reasons that do not excuse but sometimes explain how or why the abuse happened. There is always a history somewhere in any family is which abuse occurs. Reb's family had a history that probably went back many generations.

There is always a reason why the abuser does what he or she does, and often, they do not care what their actions do to others. There is a need being met by doing what they do.

When abuse happens to the very young, they have no way of knowing what is right and what isn't. Each person reacts differently and carries the scars in different ways. Some people perpetuate the abuse by becoming abusers themselves. Others strike out by becoming rebellious or striking out at others indiscriminately. In Reb's case, she held it all in, tried to survive, tried to be a good girl, as perfect as she could be, and she worked hard to create an adult world that was safe and secure, all the while burying the truth. Reb grew up during a time when there often was nowhere to turn because these things were not talked about, much less dealt with.

*   *   *

Thankfully, American society has come a long way since Reb was a child, but not far enough, not nearly far enough. Abuse continues to happen at a very high frequency and to all ages. Much of the time, it is not reported, and the perpetrator, whether of physical abuse, sexual abuse, or both, is never held accountable, and the victim is not rescued and never helped.

At the same time, bullying is in some ways an accepted part of society with only the public schools now beginning to take a stance against it. Bullying is often thought of as a part of the reality of humanity, of human civilization whether right or wrong, a reality that most of us must deal with and have endured at some point in our lives. Yet bullying is a form of abuse that should not be tolerated, not in the schools, not in the home, and not in the workplace. Bullying, sexual abuse, physical abuse, and emotional abuse are all forms of the same thing, a desire or need of the abuser with no regard for the consequence to the victim.

*   *   *

If you are an adult, whether young, middle-aged, or older, and you are being abused, leave. Just leave. Your life and your future are worth it. Help is out there.

If you are younger than the age of eighteen and you are being abused, tell the ones you trust and keep telling until someone listens and someone helps you.

Parents, you need to tell your children that there are bad things that can happen in a way that does not unduly frighten, and you need to help them know what to do if they find themselves in danger. If you have a child in your home who endangers others, face it, and lawfully and ethically do whatever is necessary to protect the other children in your home, including having the abusive child removed.

*   *   *

Schools: You have the unenviable task of addressing issues that are difficult and sensitive, and the younger the child, the more difficult and sensitive it is. You also have the task of dealing with parents who believe that they are the ones who are best suited to deal with issues about sex and safety where their children are concerned, and these parents can and do become upset when the school invades their territory. For the parents who do educate their children, they are probably right. Yet both you and I know that there are many parents who do not educate their children in matters of safety and particularly in the matter of physical and sexual abuse. Sometimes, it's because it isn't a subject that they think about; sometimes, it is because day-to-day survival takes precedence, and rarely but sometimes, it is because they or someone important to them are abusers themselves. Sometimes, it is a combination of reasons.

Yet schools have made great progress in addressing issues that were at one time considered only the providence of parents, and these changes have made a difference. What children, even very young children, have learned about topics such as fire safety, 9-1-1, nutrition, sexually transmitted diseases, birth control, etc., have changed lives for the better and have even saved lives. If Reb had had any education at all, she probably would have told.

* * *

If you are an abuser, stop. Just stop. Get help to stop what you do. If you don't stop, it is my fervent prayer that you will be caught. Get the help you need to turn your life around. Make amends to the person or people that you have hurt, at the very least acknowledging what you have done. If you don't, you deserve whatever lawful consequences or punishment you get.

* * *

Finally, if you are a young survivor or an adult survivor of any form of child abuse, know that you did nothing to cause the damage that was done to you. The guilt really is with the abuser. At the same time, it doesn't and will never give you an excuse, permission, or even a good reason for striking back. Revenge will never be the answer. More violence will never solve the problem. It will only perpetuate it. Don't let what happened to you be passed on to others. It is time to break the cycle.

*   *   *

The right kind of help is as individual as you are, but you can find it, and it may help. Facing your past and being honest with yourself is painful, is traumatic and takes courage, but it is important, and it will help. Talking to those that you trust will help. Giving yourself the time you need to heal will help. In the end, you have the ability to live the life you were meant to live in spite of the abuse.

For Reb, it took her a lifetime of more than fifty years to come to the place where she could truly live her life. It would be Reb's prayer and it is mine that you too will survive, live well, and not pass abuse onto the next generation.

CAROL ANNE LEATHERS

BOOK SUMMARY

Do Over is a story about wishing for a life different from what you have, a life different from what you have lived, and a chance to do it all over again. It is a story about childhood abuse, a woman's struggle to survive and overcome, and the belief and determination that the abuse would not be passed on to the next generation. The account of the actual abuse to the principal character Reb and her siblings is true; but the names, dates, places, and events have been fictionalized and/or changed to protect all parties. At the same time, this is a true account as to the process of living through child abuse and its long-standing consequences, if only one example, and told in story form. Thus, it is a mixture of truth and fiction.

In the end, this is a story about faith, honesty, acceptance, and love; yet it is also hoped to inspire others who have lived through their own version of the nightmare of abuse.

Autobiographical: Carol Anne Leathers lives with her husband in Maine.